The Moon Stallion

The Moon Stallion

by

Brian Hayles

fantom publishing

First published in 1978 in paperback by Mirror Books

Published in hardback in 2014 by Fantom Publishing, an imprint of Fantom Films
Reprinted in paperback by Fantom 2022
fantompublishing.co.uk

A catalogue record for this book is available from the British Library.

Paperback edition ISBN: 978-1-78196-380-7

Typeset by Phil Reynolds Media Services, Leamington Spa
Printed and bound in the UK by ImprintDigital.com

Cover design by Stuart Manning

Chapter One

IT SEEMED HARDLY ANY TIME at all since the train had laboured and protested its way through the clanking railway sidings of Didcot Junction. Now at last the iron thread of the sleepered rails had reached the hills and valleys of the Berkshire Downs, heading west, the late morning sun warming the Second Class Great Western Railway carriage.

"Is the White Horse really the biggest hill-figure in Britain?" Paul asked his father.

"It is, my boy – and probably the most ancient," came the smiled reply. Like his children, Professor Adrian Purwell was filled with a quietly bubbling anticipation, barely concealed behind his outward appearance of scholarly dignity. The White Horse of Uffington was only one of several exciting archaeological sites that they must visit. "It's of the Romano-Celtic period, certainly," he continued enthusiastically, "possibly even dating back to the Iron Age."

"Two thousand years old," said Diana brightly, "and three hundred and sixty feet long!" Her smile broadened as Paul nudged his sister in cheerful objection.

"You've been swotting it up!"

"If it was a white horse you could ride, perhaps you'd be more interested!" she teased. Paul nodded vigorously, laughing with his sister; a moment later Diana turned towards Purwell, thoughtful and questioning.

"I still don't understand what the horse means," she murmured.

"It's a picture on a hillside, that's all," asserted Paul; but, like his father, he was intrigued by her quiet intensity.

"No, Paul, it's more than that. It has to be…"

She was right, of course, brooded Purwell as he studied his daughter fondly. Behind her bright intelligence there was something more, a quality that Purwell could only call 'intuition' – an uncanny understanding of people and places, surprising in a girl of her years.

Diana smiled as she felt the warmth of the bright May sunlight on her hands. From far ahead, the engine could be heard bustling in a show of cheerful vigour as it prepared to take the long incline; the gradual slackening in the pace of the wheels over the rail joints was barely noticeable, as with a piercing blast on its whistle the engine declared its challenge. There was a slow change in direction too, setting the patch of sunlight moving fractionally along Diana's hands and bringing the acrid odour of smoke and steam drifting back along the train. It also gave Paul a chance to see the engine and carriages curving far ahead. His body twisted away from Diana, as he craned against the window, fascinated. His sister shared his excitement, but in a different, more secret fashion.

The tiny sound of her father's chased gold fob-watch snapping open brought a flicker of amusement to her lively young mouth. Both she and Paul knew that the watch was only rarely used to discover the actual time of day, but was more often a discreet gesture of suppressed excitement. Paul turned, and she could sense the grin in his voice as he spoke.

"Are we on time, Father?"

Purwell chuckled; he knew his own mannerisms well enough to be amused by Paul's familiar joke about it.

"Not far to go now," he said reassuringly. With a small nod of satisfaction, Purwell snapped the watch shut, returned it to his waistcoat pocket, and looked out at the early summer countryside rolling lazily past the carriage window. The train whistle shrilled out again, sending a grazing mare and foal breaking skittishly across the open field below the railway embankment. The foal, long-legged and ungainly, nevertheless moved with a raw grace that conjured up in Purwell's mind an ironic contrast with the grating clamour of the steam engine – muscle and sinew against steam and steel, the elegance of nature versus the brute force of industrial progress. But here, in the undulating Vale of the White Horse, that fine animal was supreme – and its grimy, smoke-belching rival had no more significance than a clockwork toy.

Paul too had seen the mare and foal, and idly watched the animals cantering across the distant field before they were lost to view. He felt restless, excited by what might lie ahead during the latest expedition organised by his father. Dry though the title 'archaeologist' might sound to Paul's schoolboy friends, his father was no ordinary, dusty professor. Digging into the past often meant almost literally that – physically lifting soil from ancient remains, frequently in far-off places. Sometimes the discoveries were nothing more than battered coins and broken pottery – but Father had an uncanny knack of stumbling across the unusual, turning a simple historical investigation into an exciting adventure, much to Paul's delight and satisfaction. Although he was almost two years younger than his sister, Paul's natural protective-ness towards her often made him seem older than he was; but this expedition had keyed him up with boyish excitement at the prospect of two pleasures in store. He would have the chance to fly his latest prize, a large, calico-covered box-kite, from the windswept heights of the Downs; and there would be opportunities to test his skills on horseback in this unfamiliar territory. It was more with this interest in mind than any thoughts of ancient history that Paul turned to his father again.

"We haven't seen the chalk horse yet," he complained.

"It isn't visible until after Uffington station," Purwell explained, half-apologetically.

"But we get off the train there," protested the dis-appointed boy. "We'll miss the chance to see it!"

"The road journey to Coleshill may give us a good view, Paul," consoled Diana, cheerfully. "But if not – will you take us there, Father?"

"It's an opportunity not to be missed," admitted the professor. "A most intriguing monument. Who made it? When? And – perhaps most important of all – why?" He smiled, dreamily. "Yes, a genuine archaeological mystery…"

"But your research for Sir George must come first," Diana reminded him, regretfully.

"I'm afraid so." He smiled at the two youngsters, his eyes shrewd and twinkling; they *would* see the White Horse if it was humanly possible, but there was someone else to be considered. "He is my patron, after all."

It had been clear to the professor from his very first meeting with Sir George Mortenhurze that he didn't suffer fools lightly. Sportsman, landowner and squire, he proved to be honest, plain-spoken and determined not to be taken for granted. He had tracked Purwell down with the tenacity of a trained hunter, and in spite of the professor's protests that lecturing commitments allowed no time for private archaeological investigations, Sir George had outlined a venture so fascinating, so close to Purwell's heart, that the archaeologist simply could not refuse. The professor was to seek out the true facts about the historical King Arthur – and in so doing, prove beyond doubt Mortenhurze's personal theory that Arthur had been a Celtic warlord who fought his last great battle on these very Berkshire hills. The fee for Purwell's expertise was to be more than generous, but the real bait was the chance to challenge history. Purwell had accepted, and the hunt was on.

The arrival at Uffington station was noisy and brief. A hissing of steam from the impatient engine, a slamming of doors, an awkward shepherding of the Purwells and their luggage and, within a minute, the guard's shrill whistle, a wave of his flag and the train was once more under way. Their tickets surrendered to the aged official, they found themselves and their luggage – including Paul's precious box-kite – waiting outside the station entrance facing a deserted yard basking in the morning sun. As the sound of the departing train faded into silence, Purwell frowned.

"Is there no one to meet us, Father?" asked Diana.

"Not yet, my dear," Purwell assured her. "But soon, no doubt."

He had no sooner spoken than into the station yard came a horse and trap in spanking trim, moving with a pace and style that showed the hand of a top-class driver. Paul stared in admiration as the trap swept round in a graceful turn, its paintwork sleek and glistening, its brass lamps and tack glittering in the sunlight.

"Isn't that splendid!" the boy exclaimed, turning to his father for agreement. Purwell nodded, impressed.

A moment later the trap had drawn up in front of them neatly and precisely, and they could see the driver clearly. He was about thirty years old, lithe and muscular, with wiry wrists and weathered hands that spoke of a taut, economical strength. Dressed not as a gentleman but with a certain smart authority, he nevertheless had a darkness to his features, a careless arrogance about his person, that suggested something wild and gypsy-like. Descending nimbly, he touched his curl-brimmed hat with token politeness and addressed himself to the children's father.

"Professor Purwell, sir?"

"You've come to take us to Coleshill Hall," Purwell acknowledged. He looked at the driver questioningly.

"Todman, sir; Sir George's stable-master," responded the driver, already summoning the sleepy porter into action with a curt gesture that ordered the bumbling lad to set the luggage at the rear of the trap.

In the same movement Todman stepped to Diana's side to hand her to her seat. Caught unprepared, she found herself being forcibly propelled forward, and, fumbling, slipped; if it hadn't been for the dark, wiry hand that took her weight, she would have fallen. Steadying herself, she wasn't to know the scorn in Todman's mind at this clumsy child who couldn't even raise her foot without falling over it. Nevertheless, she was the master's guest.

"Two steps, miss," he said, bluntly pointing out the obvious. "Take care."

Diana turned her face to him sharply, drawn not merely by the edge of insolence she had caught in his voice, but by something more unnerving, a sense of sullen, unspoken power. "I can't see them," she replied.

Todman stared into those blank, unseeing eyes and

realised for the first time that the child was blind. He frowned, as though disturbed by the fact. His lean fingers still held hers in sturdy support, and through them too he felt an awareness that this girl was… different.

"Sorry, miss," he muttered apologetically. "Didn't realise, did I?"

Paul moved forward cheerfully; he was used to saving the day from well-meaning strangers left confused by the sudden revelation of his sister's lack of sight. "I'll go first," he said; and, entering the trap in front of her, he drew Diana carefully to her place. "It's easier that way." He smiled, sitting down opposite her, his back to the driver's seat.

Purwell, clambering in after the children, nodded to Todman understandingly. "Thank you, Todman. No fault of yours."

Todman gave the older man a calm, shrewd glance that went unnoticed as the family prepared themselves for the journey ahead. With the luggage in place and checked for security, Todman tipped and dismissed the porter, then mounted the driver's seat ready to start moving. A quick glance back at his passengers assured him that all was well, though his eyes rested fractionally longer on Diana's intent face than on the others. Old words spoken over a smoking fire in the days of his boyhood came to mind, leaving him uneasy: "Twice as much, by sound and touch, knows the blind man…"

"All set there?" he called, turning to his front; in the same breath he gave a quiet chuck of his tongue that set the horse into motion. "We'll away then." A minute later the trap had left the station and the tiny village and was travelling briskly along the lanes leading to Coleshill and the Mortenhurze estate.

*

Splashed with sunlight and cool green shadows, the trap gently swooped and swerved, sped and slowed along the tangle of high-banked lanes. The railway journey, though exhilarating, had made Diana feel like a piece of luggage transported in a stuffy box; here in the open trap, without steam, smoke or engine's judder, she delighted in all the scents and sounds carried on the breeze. Close to, there was the crisp rhythm of the horse's hooves, the whisper of the wind, the tang of highly polished leather and brass; beyond that, a feeling of vast open space, humming with life. Her hand resting on her father's arm gently tightened with the sheer pleasure that she felt, and in return his gloved hand covered hers, affectionately acknowledging her delight.

"Enjoying it, my dear?" Purwell murmured, seeing the answer in Diana's face. She nodded happily.

"It's wonderful."

Paul's appreciation was typically manly and athletic. "Good riding country," he declared, glancing at Todman and hoping for some suitably sporting comment. There was no reply. The stable-master remained straight-backed and silent, all his concentration on the control of his horse, seemingly achieved by the lightest touch of fingers, wrists and reins.

Disappointed, Paul turned to speak to Diana – only to see that she was sitting bolt upright, gripping her father's arm tightly now, her face alive with excitement and alarm. Like his father, Paul froze, wondering at his sister's sudden animal-like movements as she turned this way and that, searching the hillsides about them with blind eyes, vividly aware of some strange unseen presence. When she spoke her voice was urgent but unafraid.

"Father, we must stop – now!"

Without questioning her reasons, Purwell reached across and tapped Todman's shoulder. "Todman – stop, quickly. Something's wrong!" Skilfully and in a very short distance, the trap pulled to a halt. Todman turned round to see what the trouble was, his face frowning.

"What is it, sir?" he demanded curtly.

It was Diana who answered, and now all eyes were on her blind, uptilted face. "Up there – watching us. Something strange..." As she spoke, she pointed decisively to a precise spot on the hill overlooking the lane. Puzzled and disbelieving, the others followed the direction of her gesture, wondering what it was they were supposed to see. It was Todman's sharp country-man's eyes that first saw, then narrowed in angry wonderment. It was his muttered exclamation that drew the searching gaze of the father and son closer to the mark. Above them, tossing its head proudly on the crest of the hill, stood a magnificent white stallion.

It was as though a statue, chiselled flawlessly in marble, had come to life. Todman and Paul stared at its majestic presence, fascinated; but Purwell looked back at Diana, his eyes thoughtful and questioning. She had known… but how?

"Can you see it?" she asked softly, her blind face glowing with excitement. "Tell me!"

Now Todman twisted round to study the girl's unseeing face with an almost frightening intensity that went unnoticed by Purwell, who was looking once more at the creature on the hill above them.

"It's a white stallion!" cried Paul, almost laughing with delight. "Isn't it magnificent, Father?"

"A superb specimen," murmured Purwell in agreement, then drew a small, disappointed breath as the white stallion turned away in casual arrogance and cantered out of sight over the brow of the hill.

"It's gone, hasn't it?" The excitement in Diana's face had relaxed now, and in its place was a calm, untroubled smile that touched the corners of her mouth, then crept away.

"Yes – but what a stroke of luck seeing it!" blurted Paul, his eyes still staring towards the hilltop, hoping that the horse might reappear. Purwell questioned Todman, whose feelings were carefully hidden behind a dour, emotionless expression.

"Was it a wild horse, d'you think Todman?"

"More than likely, sir," was the curt reply. The stable-master turned back to look out over the reined-in horse in the trap shafts, but his flinty eyes registered Diana's next remark with a frown as he shook the reins.

"A very special kind of wild horse…" She had spoken to herself rather than to anyone else, but the strangeness of the moment and her mood hung over all of them. It was Todman who brought the others back to the present, sourly.

"We'll go on, sir – if you don't mind." He cracked his whip lightly and the horse moved forward on the instant. "The master will be waiting."

*

Coleshill Hall was a three-storey early Regency mansion, compact but graceful, the centrepiece of a park of oak, beech and elm that even now, in early May, gave a leafy setting to the cool grey stone. A later feature of the Hall – and the most important one, under its present master – was the North Court, the stable wing designed by Mortenhurze himself to house perhaps the finest collection of thoroughbreds in England. This wing had an elegance no less commanding than the slightly larger Hall itself, a fitting comment on the status of the horse and its importance in the Mortenhurze way of life. It was a dry local saying that 'women and men who couldn't ride never shared the master's pride' at Coleshill.

A long, immaculate driveway carried the travellers through the airy grandeur of the park, straight as an arrow until it ended in a great sweeping curve before the portico steps and the canopied stone entrance of the Hall. The simply dressed but dignified figure standing there made neither sign nor movement until the trap had drawn to a halt and the horse's head was being held by the sturdy stable-boy who had been watching patiently for its return. As Todman slipped to the ground and moved to help his passengers to alight, the figure on the steps beckoned a hall-boy to deal with the luggage and then moved forward to greet Purwell and his children with a crisp but homely formality.

"Mrs Brookes, sir," she introduced herself. "The master won't be a moment. A pleasant journey, I hope?" she added with a small welcoming smile that broadened to embrace the youngsters.

"The final drive made up for all the discomforts of the train, thank you, Mrs Brookes," remarked the professor, glad to be able to stretch his legs at last. Looking all about him, Purwell saw that Todman was busy checking over the horse, while Paul had already helped his sister down from the trap before hurrying to take personal charge of his beloved kite. By now the luggage was being moved discreetly into the shaded interior of the hallway, and following its progress Purwell couldn't help but nod appreciatively at the imposing proportions of the mellowed stone façade.

Just then two figures approached from the depths of the house into the gentle May sunshine, and Purwell straightened in anticipation. Sir George Mortenhurze drew the girl walking with him closer to his side; as they confronted the Purwells there was a momentary pause.

Sir George was about forty, with a stern, hawk-like face and a physical swagger that immediately suggested a man of action. The girl by his side was about fifteen and, like her father, dressed for riding. She stood looking down at Paul and Diana with an alert, faintly commanding air, a pretty but unsmiling girl. Suddenly Mortenhurze offered his hand to Purwell and brusquely indicated his child companion.

"Morning, Professor," came the curt greeting. "My daughter, Estelle."

"Delighted, Sir George." Purwell gestured to each of his children in turn. "Diana... Paul." Even as he spoke, the professor was aware that Mortenhurze had his attention on something or someone beyond the children. He followed the squire's dark glance and caught the merest glimpse of wordless communication between Mortenhurze and the stable-master, before the squire cut the introductions short with a motion of his hand.

"Mrs Brookes will show you to your rooms," he said. "You must excuse me." In the uncomfortable pause that came next, it was the girl by Mortenhurze's side who took charge.

"I'll look after Diana," said Estelle with a sudden, winning smile. She snatched up her guest's hand and pulled her firmly into the house. "Come along!" Anxious that his sister shouldn't be hauled along too quickly, and determined not to be left out, Paul hurried in after the two girls. Purwell, finding himself summarily dismissed, had no choice but to go inside with Mrs Brookes, who obviously saw nothing unusual in her master's abrupt manner. Purwell was almost lost in the shadows of the hallway before he caught Mortenhurze's parting remark.

"We'll talk later, Professor," came the crisp, commanding voice, "over a sherry before lunch."

With that, Mortenhurze strode forward and down the steps towards Todman, who in turn curtly dismissed the waiting stable-boy, Sam. As the lad walked the horse and trap away towards the stables, Mortenhurze stood before the stable-master with an unspoken question in his eyes; but not until they were completely alone did Todman speak.

"The Moon Stallion was at Furze Hill," he said. The effect of this remark was electric; Mortenhurze stepped closer to Todman, his face flushed with barely controlled greed.

"When was this?" he demanded in a harsh whisper, his body poised and alert, yet his manner strangely secretive.

"On the way back from Uffington," Todman answered. He paused, then added deliberately, "That girl... she saw it." Mortenhurze stared at him, his eyes narrowing in disbelief.

"*Saw* it? But she's blind!"

"She knew it was there," Todman said calmly. Mortenhurze considered this, frowning anxiously. "The rest of us saw it as well," Todman added, "but *after...*"

"She can't *know*?" wondered Mortenhurze with a note of desperation in his voice.

"She's strange," said the stable-master. "Best keep her out of the way."

"A blind girl can't interfere." Mortenhurze dismissed Diana and returned obsessively to the thought of the Moon Stallion. "Furze Hill, you say?"

"You'll be wasting your time riding out there today," Todman stated flatly.

"Tomorrow then!" snapped Mortenhurze; then, even more fiercely as Todman shrugged, "We must not lose our chance!" Todman stared hard at his master; it was

Mortenhurze who stepped back, sullen-eyed.

"I've told you already, master," growled the lean-faced servant, "be patient. There's three days left to the full moon. The prize'll be ours then, you'll see."

Chapter Two

THE LIBRARY OF COLESHILL HALL was mellow and dark, its shadows filled with the rich gleam of polished mahogany panelling and bookshelves. It was a place for thought or study; yet on every wall, in every niche, there were constant and elegant reminders of Mortenhurze's most consuming passion: horses. The master of the Hall stood alone, brooding on Todman's words as he poured himself a generous glass of sherry. Moving to the fireplace, he stood with his back to the small crackling fire, oblivious of the warmth it gave to offset the coolness of these fresh May mornings. Savouring the sherry, he relaxed, comforted by the familiarity of the room and its contents. Over the mantelpiece behind him hung an oil painting of a fine stallion by Stubbs; on the opposite wall, a matching pair of framed oil sketches of horses' heads by J. F. Herring. Trophies, silver cups, small bronze statuettes of past champion hunters, mementoes of Mortenhurze's years as an officer in the regiment of cavalry... he drank again and straightened, determined to dismiss the past and its bitter memories from his mind.

Those days of early manhood has been full of pleasure and achievement; the military academy, breeding and racing horses on the estate, a perfect marriage to a lovely wife... until her death nine years ago; since then, loneliness, only partly relieved by Estelle as she grew up. The mastery of horses still gave him great satisfaction, but from this love had grown other, more dominant obsessions. The pursuit of the Moon Stallion, that living echo of Mortenhurze's greatest sadness, had become a consuming personal vendetta to be conducted in secret with only Todman's help; the other, brighter preoccupation was Arthur, that so-called Knight of the Round Table, wrapped in a clouded history of romantic fairy-tale. The quest needed expertise of a very different kind: scientific, logical, but down to earth – in short, the knowledge and skills of a practical archaeologist.

Purwell was acknowledged to be one of the best; frankly and determinedly, Mortenhurze had set out to poach the professor, snatching his services as best he could between the man's close-packed lecture tours, even though it meant acting now, in this particular month of May. Todman had given a sullen warning, but Purwell's services were available now or not at all. In the end, Mortenhurze's compulsion had won the day, and both quests now ran together in uneasy harness. Mortenhurze felt a sudden surge of annoyance, thinking about Purwell's blind daughter, then dismissed her; she was unexpected, even disturbing in her strange awareness, but surely no obstacle. Mortenhurze grew tense, remembering Todman's words. Three more nights... He drained his glass impatiently, then turned almost guiltily at the polite rap on the door. At his response, Mrs Brookes ushered Purwell into the room before quietly leaving the two men together.

Mortenhurze acknowledged Purwell's presence by pouring him some sherry and refilling his own stemmed glass.

"To an exciting investigation." Purwell sipped the aromatic wine appreciatively.

"It's the truth I'm after, Purwell," retorted Mortenhurze, countering the raised glass with his own. "No fairy tales!"

"The reality of the man we like to call 'King Arthur'," murmured the professor.

"Exactly. None of that poetic mish-mash cooked up by Tennyson and his ilk!"

"I'm an archaeologist, Sir George," Purwell reminded him.

"Precisely why I've commissioned you," came the blunt reply. "Need a practical fellow, not a bookworm." Mortenhurze gave his obviously less-than-athletic guest a dour stare. "D'you ride?"

There was no avoiding the question and Purwell could only admit the truth. "No more than passably, I'm afraid." He hurriedly offered an excuse. "With the equipment I need to carry –"

Mortenhurze cut him short with a gesture that dismissed the problem instantly. "Best provide you with a dog cart, hadn't we?"

"That would be most helpful," agreed Purwell, half-wondering if his horse-master host was secretly laughing at his guest's simple inability. In fact, Mortenhurze's suggestion was intended to be practical.

"You'll need it," he said. "There's plenty of ground to cover."

Purwell knew the area only from a detailed study of textbooks and maps, but it held out exhilarating possibilities. "These hills are full of archaeological mysteries," he agreed enthusiastically. "Standing stones – burial mounds – tumuli – sacred places linked with ancient rituals…" Even as he spoke, evocative place-names haunted the back of his mind – Liddington, Avebury, Silbury Hill, West Kenner, the Sanctuary…

"I'm not interested in that sort of nonsense," Mortenhurze declared. "This is horseman's country – Arthur's country!" He took down a rolled map from a cluttered shelf, and began to spread it out over the nearby table. "I'll show you what I mean. Here –"

He looked up, his face dark with irritation, as the library door burst open and Estelle romped in, drawing Paul and Diana with her by the hand, her face flushed with excitement.

"May we speak to you, father?" begged Estelle, her eagerness blowing away Mortenhurze's moment of anger. He turned back to the map and carefully fixed down each corner, pointedly emphasising the fact that he was engaged in serious discussion.

"If it's important, yes," he replied.

Estelle pulled Paul and Diana close to her side, so that all three could share the honour of bearing good news.

"They saw the Moon Stallion, Father," Estelle exclaimed, bright-eyed, "on their way here!"

"A rare moment – and a splendid animal," Purwell said, adding his voice in defence of the children's abrupt intrusion. Mortenhurze glanced at him dryly, then at the youngsters confronting him.

"Todman saw it first, I believe," he commented, and coolly resumed his perusal of the map. He didn't notice Diana's frown at his remark, or the small, questioning turn of her head towards Paul, standing close by. But Estelle already had Paul's attention, as she pouted in cheerful disappointment at not being the very first with this rare piece of information.

"He's already told you?"

"Of course," retorted her father. "He knows my interest in the creature."

"I thought Paul might show me where tomorrow," suggested Estelle, not to be outdone.

"Furze Hill, as it happens," Mortenhurze informed her, nodding agreeably. "I shall ride there with you – to see for myself."

I thought you might," smiled his daughter, pleased that he had fallen in with her suggestion. Bringing the news of the Moon Stallion hadn't been wasted after all.

"Arrange about mounts with Todman, will you?"

instructed Mortenhurze. He glanced at Diana uncertainly, then threw a silent question at the girl's father. Purwell shook his head in answer, appreciating his patron's consideration, and Mortenhurze continued, "Yours and mine, and something suitable for the boy." Estelle didn't need telling twice. Eagerly ushering Paul and Diana out of the room, she gave her father a quick smile of thanks.

"I'll arrange it now!" she cried, closing the door after her with exaggerated care. Purwell couldn't help smiling at the child's infectious gaiety, but Mortenhurze firmly drew his attention back to the map.

"It's there before you, Purwell – see for yourself!" Purwell's finger found and traced the line of the ancient track that ran for miles along the crest of the chalk hills.

"The Ridgeway," he identified, "and here –" his finger pinpointed a series of clearly marked symbols, "– the great hill forts." The Roman roads were there, too, as were the mystical centres of Avebury and Stonehenge; but, Purwell realised, the map only showed the lower half of England and the Wessex Downs. "To my knowledge," he pointed out, "Arthur's reported victories are scattered all over early Britain."

Mortenhurze had clearly expected this objection, and was ready for it. "The Celts were first-class horsemen," he retorted, "as you probably know."

Purwell agreed. "These hills were renowned for breeding and racing horses, even in A.D. 500," he admitted.

"Let me tell you what horses meant to Arthur,"

insisted Mortenhurze. "A force that could strike at speed, disrupt enemy supply lines and cover enormous distances to give battle when needs be!" His eyes challenged the professor to deny his next remark. "And these hills – the Vale of the White Horse, down to Pewsey – these were the very heart of his defences!"

"Arthur the Celtic warlord…" mused Purwell. "A long way removed from romantic legends of Tintagel and the Knights of the Round Table."

The simplicity and directness of Mortenhurze's bold concept appealed to him strongly; but proving that Arthur was in fact a Celtic Imperator of Horse, leading native resistance against the Saxons, wouldn't be easy.

"It challenges tradition," he stated keenly, "and I welcome that. But where do we begin?"

"With Arthur's battles." Mortenhurze jabbed at the map, confidently. "And most important of all – Mount Badon!"

"His greatest victory," said Purwell, frowning, "but it has never been firmly located."

"That battle is the key," Mortenhurze claimed, with total confidence, "and I'm certain it happened in these hills!"

Purwell looked back at the map, his mind lost in a daydream of glorious discovery. "Mount Badon," he murmured. "If we could unearth *that*…!"

Mortenhurze's reply was typically blunt, demanding proof, not idle speculation. "Well? You're the archaeologist. Go out and find it!"

*

"Paul," asked Diana thoughtfully, "*was* Todman the first to actually see the Moon Stallion?"

They were outside now, moving through the sunny, formal gardens at the back of the house, on their way to the stables. Estelle was slightly ahead, leading the way, while Paul took more care, guiding his sister by the hand through this unknown territory.

"Yes," replied Paul casually, "I suppose he was. Why do you ask?" Before Diana could reply, Estelle came running back to them, cheerfully impatient at their progress.

"The stables are this way!" she cried. "Come on!"

"Estelle…" Diana held out her hand to summon the cheerful girl to her side. "I wanted to ask you –"

"Am I wearing you out?" laughed Estelle, adding even before Diana could protest, "Let's sit here for a moment!" Helped to the nearby bench, Diana sat with Estelle by her side. Paul stood close by, taking in the mathematical elegance of the balustrades, flowerbeds and lawns sweeping down to a carefully designed sprawl of shrubbery and trees. For a moment, all three youngsters were silent, breathing in the early summer fragrance of the peaceful scene. Diana seemed to have forgotten her question, but Paul was quickly restless once again.

"Do you think we stand a chance of seeing that wild stallion again tomorrow?" he asked Estelle.

"It happens so rarely," she replied, a little enviously. "You were very lucky to see it at all!"

"Have *you* ever seen it, Estelle?" queried Diana, her

24

face shadowed with a quiet concern.

"Never," came the frank reply. "I was too young, the last time it appeared."

Paul was intrigued. "How long ago was that?"

"Nine years." It was Diana who had answered, and Estelle stared at her in sharp surprise.

"Yes, it was… but how could you know?" she asked.

Diana knew she could offer no easy explanation; whatever she said was bound to sound strange or silly. "Some things… happen in that kind of pattern," she murmured lamely. "In a sort of… natural cycle." Before Estelle could attempt to puzzle this out, Paul tried to turn the subject back to the horse.

"Was it the same stallion? Didn't anyone ever try to catch it?" he demanded.

A gentle, dreamy sadness softened Estelle's bright face, as she ignored Paul's question and lost herself in remembering that distant fragment of time.

"It was during May," she recalled, "this very month. I was only six, but I remember…" She paused for a shadowed moment, then went on with a fondness in her voice that wasn't there before. "She told me… how beautiful the stallion looked – gleaming in the moonlight like sky-silver…" For a second, the others were caught up in the sad serenity of Estelle's remembering; it was Paul who at last broke the mood, gently insistent.

"Who told you that? Who saw it?" he asked.

"My mother," was the simple direct answer. "She died that midsummer."

Diana's hand reached out and found Estelle's in a

small, silent gesture of understanding. Grateful, Estelle took the proffered hand in both her own, and in the tiny silence that followed, no one moved. Then, as Paul valiantly mumbled an apology for his clumsy question, Estelle tried to lift the mood from them with a cheerful smile.

"Don't worry – it was a long time ago," she said, then added in a mock-gossipy aside, "Some people said it was the old superstition coming true!" But the smile faded, to be replaced by a shadow of quiet alarm behind her eyes when Diana spoke next, in a strange, dreamy chant.

"Who sees the stallion in the moonlit shoon…" She stopped; then, as Paul looked on, wondering, Estelle solemnly picked up where Diana had left off, and completed the tag.

"… sees never another a harvest moon." With a quick, bright laugh, she broke the dark mood, but her eyes were fixed on the blind girl's face, begging for an answer. "You are strange, Diana – knowing that old rhyme. Did Mrs Brookes tell it to you?" Diana's flat reply only served to puzzle Estelle more deeply.

"No."

"Diana often surprises us like that," Paul tried to explain. "Knowing things… understanding…" He decided to turn the issue into a joke. "You know – the way cats can tell the weather, in advance!"

Both the girls smiled, but Estelle was still intrigued. "They have a sixth sense, don't they?" she remarked.

"Coincidence, more often than not!" laughed Diana, the strangeness about her quite gone.

"Father doesn't like mysteries," claimed Estelle, standing up, ready to move on. "He says the Moon Stallion's only a wild horse, and that one day he'll take it for his very own!"

Now it was Diana's turn to frown in quiet alarm, but the expression went unnoticed as the others pulled her to her feet.

"What a prize that would be!" exclaimed Paul. Estelle nodded in agreement, as she drew brother and sister onward eagerly.

"Come to the stables," she insisted, "and see the horses we *have* got, the best in all England!"

*

In the stable yard, Todman's experienced hands and keen glance had finished checking over a gelding held by Sam; the stable-master stepped back, satisfied, but even as he waved the horse away to its stall, he watched its every movement with narrowed, thoughtful eyes. Following its leisurely, graceful progress, Todman frowned – not at the horse, but at the tight cluster of young visitors who had entered the yard. They stood admiring the gelding as it passed them, and were in no way a hindrance; there was no complaint that Todman could make, except that, as before, the blind girl standing across the yard from him with such attentive stillness left him with a feeling of unease. The feeling was instinctive; it couldn't be explained, but Todman heeded it – and almost immediately suppressed it beneath an expression of polite enquiry, as Estelle led her companions towards him.

27

"Yes, miss?" he asked, touching the brim of his hat respectfully.

"Father would like three mounts ready for tomorrow morning, please, Todman," Estelle informed him. Todman's glance flicked onto Diana.

"Three, miss?"

Estelle explained, slightly impatient. "Rollo for Father, Rex for me – and something sensible for Paul, here."

"I see, miss," responded Todman, relaxing and looking Paul over appraisingly. The lad looked sturdy enough. "Ridden much, Master Purwell?" he asked politely.

"Quite a bit," answered Paul keenly, not wanting to be taken for a complete dunce. In fact, he was more than passable, with strong hands. "Don't give me a hack, will you?" he pleaded with a smile.

"We don't have any such animals in these stables, sir," Todman answered, calmly reproving. "You'll have one that'll suit you, don't worry."

"And I'd like you to walk Duchess," Estelle interrupted, "to show Diana."

Todman struggled not to show the unease that rose from deep within him. "*Show* her, miss?"

"I'll know how she stands... by touch," Diana said confidently. Estelle grew enthusiastic.

"She really is a beauty – one of our prize mares!" She was cut short by Todman's polite but flat refusal.

"I'd rather not, miss."

"What?" Estelle's face flushed with anger, and her

voice cracked like a whip, but Todman stood his ground.

"Duchess won't be happy, miss," the stable-master carefully explained. "She don't like anything... unusual." His glance briefly indicated Diana's black, unseeing eyes, but he gave a more discreet reason: "Like being touched by strangers."

Next to her father, Estelle was mistress of Coleshill Hall, and not used to being disobeyed – least of all in front of guests and friends. The temper she had inherited from her father showed now in the icy, controlled command she gave to Todman. "You will do as I say!" she snapped.

He responded immediately. "Very well, miss." He moved quickly across the yard to the stall that housed Duchess. Estelle, feeling more than a little pleased at her successful show of authority, took Paul and Diana by the arms to a position where they could see and hear the fine mare which was to be brought out for their inspection, but Paul was concerned.

"*Is* Duchess temperamental?" he asked, glancing at Diana protectively.

"Never!" insisted Estelle emphatically. "It's just that Todman gets rather touchy about who's allowed to pet her, you see." She looked at the horse proudly. "She *is* rather special."

Paul had to agree as Todman, his hand on the splendid mare's halter, brought her out of her stall and into the yard. Graceful, dignified and calm, Duchess slowly walked forward towards the youngsters; Paul stepped to one side, next to Estelle, to view the fine beast more clearly. In doing so, he left Diana isolated and waiting quietly alone in the corner of the yard, as Todman and the mare moved between her and the others. The blind girl turned her head, intently following the sounds of the advancing animal – her hooves on the cobbles of the yard, the quiet blowing of the mare as she paused, majestically, her master at her head. In the same moment Todman, reassuringly stroking the mare's massively arched neck, glanced coldly at the unseeing girl nearby and murmured a command into the horse's finely pricked ear.

The whisper – and his hand letting go of the halter – went unnoticed in the frightening confusion that followed. The mare seemed to explode in a welter of lashing hooves, neighing in wild panic as she tore free of Todman and reared, a terrifying mass of rippling muscle, high over Diana. Instinctively, Paul and Estelle had scrambled out of range of those fearsome hooves, but the neighing, terrified mare seemed to see only Diana, now backed tightly against the corner of the yard. Helpless but strangely unafraid, the blind girl stood silent and unmoving, as though unaware of the flurry of steel-tipped hooves that threatened only inches from her defenceless head.

"Todman! Get Duchess away!" screamed Estelle in helpless alarm, while Paul watched desperately for the chance to spring to his sister's side, prevented by those vicious, terrifying hooves.

"Diana, don't move!" he shouted. "Stay still!"

Pressed hard back against the wall, Diana could

barely hear her brother's urgent cry above the threshing and screaming of the frantic mare; but, understanding his meaning, she nodded calmly, unafraid and perfectly still.

"I'm all right, Paul," she called, but her voice was lost in the flurry of wild sound. Beyond her brother and Estelle, Todman stood poised, making no move to interfere, his eyes fixed with intense concentration on Diana – until Estelle's desperate voice shrilled out again, and he acted, swift as a swooping hawk.

"Todman – for heaven's sake, take her! Quickly!"

In two strides the stable-master had ducked under the lunging hooves and snatched at the dangling halter. In the split second that Duchess came to the ground before rearing up again, Todman murmured another soft command into the mare's ear – and in that instant, she was calm. Fondling the beast's sweating head, the stable-master looked across at the blind girl as Paul and Estelle ran anxiously to her side, and he frowned.

"Diana – are you all right?" demanded her brother.

"Duchess has never acted like that before!" Estelle could not hide her dismay. "It was terrifying!"

"She didn't frighten me," Diana reassured them gently, then added with quiet concern, "I think she's the one who needs looking after."

Duchess stood patient and calm again, as though the incident had never happened. It had only taken seconds, Todman reckoned, but it had proved who was master. He patted the mare's muzzle, and addressed Estelle firmly.

31

"Best if I take her in, miss," he said.

"Yes," his young mistress responded reluctantly, "do that, Todman." Grudgingly, she allowed him the respect that his cool assurance demanded. "And I'm sorry – you were right."

He nodded politely, and, turning to lead the mare inside, permitted himself a small, arrogant smile which he knew the youngsters could not see...

Chapter Three

THE NEXT MORNING WAS FRESH and sparkling, as Purwell stood in the shaded portico with his daughter, waving to the three riders walking their horses towards the open parkland and the ride beyond. Diana could only listen to the intricate rhythm of hoof-beats on the gravelled drive as they quickened and faded into the distance, but her father noted with some pride that Paul was more than up to the occasion. Casual but immaculately dressed, the boy sat his horse well; only the experienced eye could tell at this point that Paul has spent relatively little time learning the skills of riding, whereas Estelle had been schooled to the sport from the tender age of three.

The horses walked on, blowing nervously, eager to be worked and eventually given their head on the open hills. Mortenhurze, in the lead, gave Purwell and Diana only the barest of formal acknowledgement, as befitted his status as Master of the Hunt. Paul, riding at the rear of his host alongside Estelle, gave a more cheery, slightly mischievous wave, before breaking into a gentle canter and riding away. Purwell watched Diana's bright unseeing wave gradually falter as the departing horses were lost to view across the bright shimmer of parkland.

He stopped waving and, holding her arm, stood for a lingering moment, taking in the sunny welcome of the May morning. Her quiet face was gently uptilted to the almost cloudless sky as though drinking in its promise of greater warmth to come; she seemed quite untouched by yesterday's alarming incident, described so graphically to Purwell by his son. Diana had seemed more concerned about just how Todman had controlled the frenzied horse than the fact that her life had been in real danger. Thankful that the event was past and that Diana had come to no harm, he gave her arm an affectionate squeeze, and led the way into the cool recesses of the house.

The ride over the hills was sheer pleasure for Paul. The mount that Todman had picked out for him was responsive but sensible, always taking a line that offered pace and excitement without putting Paul – or the horse – in difficulty. With the practised eye of a master horseman, Mortenhurze had quickly realised Paul's limitations, and deliberately chose one of the less testing routes that would take them past Furze Hill and Barrowbush Hill to swing in a gentle arc along the high ground of the Vale, past the villages of Uffington, Woolstone and Compton Beauchamp. This pleasantly picturesque ride wasn't designed merely to entertain the young visitor, however; these were the downlands where the Moon Stallion had been seen and would be seen again, at the fated time. This was the sole reason for Mortenhurze's presence, and he wasted no time in casual conversation; idle chatter was left to Estelle as hostess, while her father studied the hillsides all about them with the keen concentration of the hunter. He rode straight-backed and alert, using knees and hands sparingly, totally at one with Rollo, his favourite chestnut. Estelle, like Paul, rode for the sheer physical enjoyment of the gallop, exchanging laughter and merry comments half-lost on the wind as she and Paul played at a form of chase or tag, making sure their high spirits never bothered her father, riding so sternly ahead.

It was with some surprise, then, that they found Mortenhurze had reined his horse to a halt, and stood waiting for the youngsters to ride up to his side. The explanation lay in the brusque gesture he gave, indicating the view high to their left. Paul looked up and was entranced, while Estelle, who had seen that majestic hillside so many times before, smiled at his obvious wonderment. There, crisp white against green turf sharpened by the bright May sunshine, was the White Horse of Uffington – immense, unmoving, yet alive.

The great chalk image of the horse dominated the shadowed flank of the lofty hill; a single, fluid line ran from nose to tail, a line vibrant with leaping power. From that flowing form sprang two main legs, the hind leg thrusting to the rear, a fore leg reaching out to the front, beyond the strangely beaked head. Two other legs were indicated, both free of the lean body, and below the deep cleft of the ears was set a large round eye. The immediate impact of the image was at once crudely barbaric yet strangely elegant.

"It's enormous!" exclaimed Paul, but then his wondering face frowned in puzzlement. "But it doesn't look like a horse at all!"

Before Estelle could offer explanation or argument, she turned sharply at the sound of her father's sudden bark of excitement.

"I see it!" he cried out, harshly. "There – over there!"

The youngsters looked to where Mortenhurze had pointed; but he was already riding away at a furious gallop, lashing his horse into a mighty effort to reach what he had seen on the hillside crest topping the far side of the valley. Standing there, quite motionless, was the mysterious white stallion.

"The Moon Stallion!" Paul shouted in delight.

"Father, wait!" Estelle wheeled her horse about and desperately followed Mortenhurze; Paul, determined not to be left out, rode after them, but was left trailing far behind in the wake of Mortenhurze's swift impassioned charge. Estelle, however much she tried, couldn't gain on her father's horse; Rollo's great strides seemed to devour the ground beneath him, and even against the pull of the slope he began to come tantalisingly close to the Moon Stallion on the crest above. But the strange white horse was not waiting to be taken. With a toss of his flowing mane, he turned gracefully and casually away, and was lost to sight over the brow of the hill.

Still Mortenhurze rode on furiously, his face dark with obstinate determination. Nothing else in the world existed for him but that wild white horse, and it was almost within his grasp. But at the crest, there was nothing. Reining in his horse savagely, he turned this way and that, looking all about him, tense with frustration, desperate to see where the Moon Stallion had gone. It had vanished. The slopes and combes around him were utterly deserted; the only sounds were the thudding hoof-beats of the youngsters' horses, approaching under the mocking whisper of the gentle wind.

When Paul and Estelle reached the hilltop, they found Mortenhurze sitting hunched in his saddle like an embittered hawk robbed of its prey. Silently, he glowered over the empty hillside, and Paul shared his disappointment. Estelle, gently questioning her father, seemed relieved.

"Where to now, Father?"

"We've lost it," came his terse reply. He straightened, and instinctively patted Rollo's neck, commending the animal's mighty effort in the pursuit. Mortenhurze had stopped his narrow-eyed searching now, but Estelle still kept up the pretence, in a brave show of sympathy.

"Where could it go?" she asked, her question drifting on the wind.

"Not a sign of it," moodily observed Paul. "It's completely disappeared,"

"Like a damned ghost!" grated Mortenhurze angrily

to himself. Failure gnawed at him like a physical pain. Paul, unaware of the intensity of Mortenhurze's dark obsession, turned to him, fresh-faced and eager, only to find himself put in the place by a cold, flinty glare.

"*Was* it the Moon Stallion, sir?"

"It was a wild horse, boy – nothing more!" was the short reply. Mortenhurze turned away, seething with quiet fury. "And I *will have it!*"

With that, he brought his horse about and slowly and stiffly cantered down and across the slope, heading homewards. The youngsters followed him, the brightness of their morning faded, passing on their disconsolate way an insignificant clump of briar-screened trees that filled a small hollow in the slope. Even had they looked, it is unlikely they would have seen what was hidden there: an unmoving glimmer of white, so still it might have been a marble statue…

*

"A fine capture, if you'd managed it," commented Purwell, watching his host pour himself a drink, a morning luxury that the professor had politely declined.

"It was a close-run thing, I can tell you," growled Mortenhurze, reluctant to embroider the event. He would have said even less, but Estelle, full of excitement over what had happened, had blurted out the details to Purwell and his daughter almost as soon as she had returned from the morning ride, still breathless.

"Was it the same horse?" asked Diana.

"Paul thinks so," answered Estelle, speaking for him; he had stayed with the horses, eager to be involved with the elaborate ritual of unsaddling and grooming after the ride – a request surprisingly granted by Todman, who had apparently decided to take the boy under his wing.

"It *has* to be the same horse," Diana murmured to herself, unaware of Mortenhurze's sharp, sidelong glance as he heard her quiet remark.

"Are there many wild horses in these hills, Sir George?"

Purwell's innocent interest drew Mortenhurze's attention back to him. "A small number, yes." A glint of memory brightened his face, as he recalled that first quick sighting of the Moon Stallion. "But only one with that colouring and stature."

"Something of a rarity then," suggested Purwell.

"There has always been a White Horse, Father." Diana's flat declaration brought the conversation to an awkward, uneasy standstill; in the small silence that followed, Mortenhurze stared at the blind girl over his drink, irritated and disturbed by her interruption. Sensing her father's mood, Estelle tried to explain away the mystifying comment.

"If you mean the chalk horse," she cut in brightly, "that's centuries old!"

"I meant the stallion as well." This direct and puzzling response added to the irritation that Mortenhurze could no longer contain.

"What's the girl talking about, Purwell?" he demanded. "Sheer nonsense!"

The professor looked at his daughter, thoughtfully; making nonsensical remarks simply wasn't in her nature

– he sometimes wished it was. But what exactly *was* her meaning?

"A legendary connection, perhaps," Purwell commented mildly.

"That's more like it!" laughed Estelle. "Real horses don't live even as long as humans do," she reasoned brightly, "so it can't have been the identical animal every time!"

Purwell was suddenly more interested; here was something he hadn't known about. "The stallion has been seen on these hills before?"

"Oh, several times – so they say…" Estelle floundered, aware from her father's face that she may have said too much.

"Every nine years," came Diana's quiet voice.

"There have been reports," admitted Mortenhurze, coldly dismissive. "Hearsay, mostly."

"Why is it called the Moon Stallion?" queried Purwell pleasantly, trying to steer the conversation towards a more general subject and so ease Mortenhurze's obvious irritation. "Is there some superstition attached to it?" he continued amiably. "Some local custom, perhaps?"

"Nothing related to archaeological fact, Professor," said Mortenhurze flatly. "Nothing but old wives' tales." His terse comment, far from ending the conversation as was intended, seemed to trigger off a deep, insistent voice in Diana's mind. She heard a dreamy, insistent voice – and suddenly knew that it was her own, reciting.

"Who sees the stallion in moonlit shoon
Sees never another harvest moon."

The voice stopped. Estelle, seeing her father stiffen as though resisting pain, caught her breath in silent dismay.

"You would do well to disregard the gossip of servants, Miss Purwell," Mortenhurze commented icily.

"*I* told her, Father," Estelle bravely admitted. The chilling edge of her father's disapproval now turned against Estelle. Guiltily, she accepted his quiet, almost whispered rebuke, her sad face bowed submissively.

"Have you *no* consideration for my feelings?"

Estelle fought back her rising misery; she hated it when her father was so deeply hurt and angry. She silently resolved not to let him down again, as Purwell's dry voice tried to break the shadowed moment.

"Quite a common rural superstition, the beast of ill-fortune," he observed, chattily. "Herne the Hunter, for example." The name went unrecognised, and he hastened to explain. "A ghostly figure said to haunt Windsor Great Park."

"This horse is real!" Mortenhurze flatly insisted, and now Estelle sprang to his defence.

"Of course it is," she affirmed cheerfully. "It's been seen two days running, now – by all of us – *and* in broad daylight! How *can* it be a ghost?"

Mortenhurze had had enough. Determined to bring the conversation to an end, he took Diana by the hand and drew her to her feet.

"You see, Miss Purwell," he said, pleasantly decisive,

41

"there is no mystery about the horse and no earthly need for morbid speculation." He glanced pointedly towards Purwell, and continued shrewdly, "Your father has work to do – and I suggest the morning air will clear these… cobwebs… from your mind."

Purwell moved towards the door with a small guilty smile. "I shall work in the library until lunch, Diana," he informed her. "Perhaps you'd like a walk in the garden, with Estelle?" He nodded, and was gone.

Estelle questioned the blind girl gently. "Shall we, Diana?" Diana nodded, pleased; but now Mortenhurze interrupted.

"Estelle, your guest might find it chilly outside," he remarked. "Fetch her a shawl, won't you?"

"Of course," Estelle answered promptly, and gave Diana's arm a small, reassuring squeeze. "I shan't be a moment!"

She was gone, and Mortenhurze and Diana were alone together; suddenly Diana was aware that this had been her host's intention all along. She waited for him to speak, but he said nothing. She sensed he was watching her closely; the hand that still held hers was firm and strong, but no longer tense and angry. Was he waiting for Diana to speak?

"Please don't be angry with Estelle," she murmured, "it was my fault."

"You weren't to know." His reply was calm now, but with a deeper undertone that only Diana's senses could detect. "But Estelle was thoughtless." He paused, and then went on as though compelled to explain. "There are memories… too painful, even now…"

"Even after nine years…" Diana murmured.

Mortenhurze, intent on explaining, didn't seem to hear. "I'd hoped… prayed… that Estelle would forget." The tension returned as a tremor to his hand, and his next words were barely audible. "I cannot."

For a split second, Diana knew and understood his sadness. "You must try," she said gently. She could offer him no consolation that his pride would allow him to accept. She was only a child, and he distrusted her; she realised that she risked his anger with her words. She felt his anguish tighten the grip on her hand almost to the point of pain, but she barely flinched as she sensed him fighting for control of his feelings.

The door opened, and Estelle came running to them, a light shawl in her hand. Mortenhurze released Diana, and withdrew from the two girls. He poured himself another drink, his face composed now.

"You might start by showing Diana the conservatory, my dear," he suggested, then, drink in hand, took a step closer to Estelle as she placed the shawl about Diana's shoulders.

"Yes, Father," she agreed, then wondered at the moment of hesitation in his voice.

"And Estelle –" he started. He couldn't go on; the need to apologise was almost agonising. Soft words and sentiment never came easily to Mortenhurze. Instead, a brief pressure on Estelle's slim shoulder was all he could manage – but it was enough, and with a quick smile, the girl showed she understood, and left happily with Diana.

BRIAN HAYLES

Alone, Mortenhurze could feel the unease inside him rising again; there was a feeling that he was standing on quicksand, that events were slipping out of his control. Only one person could give him reassurance: Todman. Finishing his drink at a gulp, Mortenhurze strode from the room and headed purposefully towards the stables.

*

Paul stood watching Todman deftly remove saddle and tack from Rollo, the master's favourite, a task invariably reserved for the stable-master himself.

"I'm not surprised that Sir George wants the Moon Stallion for his own," Paul commented, still excited about the morning's chase.

"So would any horseman," retorted Todman dourly, "if he could catch it."

"That won't be easy." Paul paused, recalling the swiftness of its disappearance. "It runs like the wind!"

"It can be taken," was the flat reply.

"The way you managed Duchess yesterday?" asked Paul, admiringly.

"Horses know me," stated Todman. "I talk, and they listen." He smiled, thinly. "We'd get on well, that wild horse and me." Todman moved around the horse, with Paul trailing at his heels.

"Is the stallion really a wild horse?" he asked.

"What else would it be?" countered the stable-master sharply, putting Paul on the defensive.

"Perhaps it's run loose from someone's stable –"

"Not that one."

"Then there could be others like him up there?"

44

"There's been horses on these hills for centuries, Master Purwell," grunted Todman. Everything bar the halter had now been stripped from the chestnut, and it only remained for a Newmarket to be flung over the fine back.

"I know – Father told me," Paul said knowledgeably. "They were bred for fighting battles – by the Celtic tribes here."

"And for racing, too."

"Running horse festivals," smiled Paul. "D'you think the chalk horse was the finishing post?"

Todman threw the boy a sober look. "Don't joke," he rebuked casually. "That creature has more meaning than any of us knows…"

Paul saw a possibility unhinted at by Diana. "Could the White Horse have something to do with King Arthur and his battles, then?" he asked eagerly.

"That's for the professor to find out, isn't it?" Todman retorted as he left the stall, closing the half-door, with Paul behind him carrying a few small items of tack.

"I'd much rather hunt for the Moon Stallion, myself," said the boy, following Todman to the tackroom, along the line of stalls.

"You won't see that one again in a hurry," muttered the stable-master.

"Couldn't we try?"

Todman looked at the boy thoughtfully. "You don't catch a hare with a drum," he said.

"At least show me where the horse festivals were

held," begged the youngster. "Please?"

Todman laid out the used tack to be inspected and cleaned. His sidelong glance was sharp, though his voice was pleasant enough. "Not without your dad's permission," he insisted. Paul's face lit up with pleasure.

"I'll ask him – now!" he blurted out. "On the Downs – tomorrow morning?"

"Could be."

"Hurray!" Paul exclaimed, laughing with excitement. "And I promise not to tempt providence by saying what we're *really* looking for!"

He burst out of the tackroom door and sprinted across the stable yard, narrowly avoiding a collision with Mortenhurze. The boy stumbled to a breathless halt, fixed by Mortenhurze's stern stare.

"Careful, boy!"

"Sorry, sir." Mortenhurze accepted the apology with a nod, and Paul nimbly skipped past him, running towards the house. Mortenhurze watched him go. Then he turned back to Todman, now standing in the tackroom doorway.

"Being a nuisance, is he?"

"Gone to ask his dad if he can ride over White Horse Hill tomorrow," explained the stable-master.

Mortenhurze responded sharply, alarm in his voice. "He must not be allowed to interfere!"

"He won't," said Todman. "I'll be riding with him."

The squire's face showed his surprise and confusion. Couldn't Todman see that the boy was a threat, an intruder? "But why on earth…?" Mortenhurze demanded.

Todman studied his master, weighing his words carefully. "Suppose *he's* the chosen one?" he said, calmly meeting his master's troubled eyes with a tilt of the head.

"It isn't possible," protested Mortenhurze; but the point had been scored.

"Twice it's happened now," Todman went on. "He's been there – seen it – both times."

"Fluke!" muttered his master, "sheer coincidence."

"It could happen again," Todman added, pointedly. "Third time lucky."

Unease and alarm rippled through Mortenhurze, slowly, unnervingly. "The boy can't be... another whisperer?" He gripped Todman's shoulder. "No one else but you – that was your claim!" Todman met his master's eyes unflinchingly.

"If he has the power, he doesn't know it." Todman saw his master was still disturbed, and wondered at his fear.

"The girl is different," Mortenhurze explained. "She understands... something."

Todman shrugged the hand from his shoulder angrily, and Mortenhurze stepped back as though acknowledging who was the true master. "I told you to keep her from crossing my path, didn't I?" Todman grated fiercely. "She must not interfere! Nor her father!"

"I can only try and divert them –" lamely offered Mortenhurze. Todman was not placated; his eyes glinted dangerously.

"Make sure you do!"

Chapter Four

"Whatever his beginnings," said the professor, "Arthur eventually became much more than just a local hero. He was celebrated as far afield as France and even Italy!"

"The ideal of romantic chivalry," murmured Diana, "the perfect, holy knight in shining armour."

The day was drawing to its close; with Mortenhurze and his daughter away for the afternoon, tea had been served in the library to enable Purwell to continue his researches there without pause, and his children had joined him from the garden. By now Paul had demolished most of the cucumber sandwiches single-handed and, between mouthfuls, was looking over his father's shoulder at the several maps strewn over the library table. Inevitably, the subject of Arthur had been raised, giving Paul and Diana the chance to enjoy

Purwell's natural enthusiasm.

"I always thought he was best known in the West Country," commented Paul, "but that's hardly shown on this map at all."

"Sir George isn't interested in the inventions of chroniclers like Geoffrey of Monmouth, my boy," smiled Purwell. "Names like Camelot and Tintagel have a ring to them, I grant you; but hard fact is more difficult to come by, I'm afraid." He chuckled, drily. "Even the report that Arthur's bones were found at Glastonbury in the twelfth century needs a pinch of salt."

"Why's that, Father?" asked Paul as he gobbled the last tiny sandwich.

"Pilgrims," explained his father. "Holy bones drew visitors – and money to help restore the abbey."

"It was a splendid story, though, Father," said Diana.

"A fine entertainment, certainly," replied Purwell. "Wonderful adventures; wonderful names, too: Tintagel, Merlin, Excalibur, the magic sword, and the dying Arthur, carried away to Avalon, the mysterious Isle of the Dead…"

"And the battles, Father," Paul reminded him. "Don't forget them!"

"Even more dubious," chuckled Purwell. "Do you realise that according to Geoffrey's chronicle, Arthur not only conquered the Saxons, but Ireland, Iceland, Norway *and* Gaul as well?"

"What about the Round Table, though?" persisted Paul. "Didn't you tell us once that it's exhibited for everyone to see at Winchester?"

"There is *a* table, certainly," agreed his father, "and looking at it, I'd say it was extremely old." He eyed Paul shrewdly, and gave a wry smile. "Made about the same period that the legend of the Round Table was invented, I'd say – about six or seven hundred years after Arthur died."

"Not all the stories are to do with chivalry and courtly love, are they, Father?" asked Diana.

"Indeed not, my dear," Purwell responded. "Arthur was sometimes linked with an ancient god who slept in a magic cave somewhere in the Western Isles, wherever they may be. Not only that," he added, "Arthur was said to be one of the fairy people, a giant-killer, and even able to turn himself into a raven, riding the clouds!"

"Arthur wasn't a god," Diana said with a frown. "He wasn't a magician, either."

"Of course he wasn't," agreed the professor. "A hero, certainly – quite possibly a commander of cavalry, as Sir George insists."

"Arthur must have been a master horseman, too," declared Paul, adding admiringly, "like Todman."

"Perhaps Todman has Celtic ancestors!" Purwell suggested.

"He looks more like a gypsy to me," Paul reflected, then turned to Diana to answer the question that cut across their moment of good humour.

"Paul," she asked, "tell me again what Todman did to make Duchess calm again."

Paul willingly obliged. "It was amazing. He simply murmured something to it – and the horse stopped thrashing around immediately!"

Diana's face clouded, her solemn mood in contrast to Paul's excited admiration.

"I think he could be a horse whisperer," she said.

"A horse whisperer?" echoed Paul, amused. "What sort of trade is that?"

His father supplied the information cheerfully, but his eyes rested thoughtfully on Diana. "It's a term going back ages," he commented. "Some horse handlers were so skilful they were thought to use magic words or witchcraft to control their animals." He paused, then went on, "But that superstition died centuries ago."

"Magic and horses have always been linked, haven't they, Father?" Diana insisted.

"True," admitted Purwell, "there used to be running horse festivals at the feast of Beltane, in these very hills."

"Todman knew about the ancient racing," remarked Paul, intrigued, "but he didn't mention Beltane. Which one's that?"

"The Celtic May Day," Diana answered.

"What were they celebrating?"

It was Purwell who responded. "They were trying to ensure a good harvest and fertile stock, my boy. A ritual dedicated to life and continuity." He went on, sombrely, "There were great jollifications, of course – but there was a darker side. They lit great bale-fires to ward off death and evil… and there were human sacrifices, too."

"They sound a bit savage, I must say," said Paul.

"We forget how much, now that we've adapted their primitive feast days and given them new names," nodded

Purwell. "Their great New Year feast on November the first, for instance. We call it All Saints' Day, now."

"And we keep their bonfires, too," Diana pointed out. "Hallowe'en, and Guy Fawkes –"

"To drive away evil spirits?" asked Paul.

"And a memory of ancient sacrifice, at a time when the barriers between the living and the dead were at their weakest." Purwell smiled, reassuringly. "A time for ghosts and witches... and children's parties!"

"Is that how the horse races fitted into Beltane?" Paul's interest was stirred. "As games?"

"The horses were raced in honour of Epona." Diana's quiet voice was soft, but it penetrated the darkening shadows of the room. Paul questioned the name.

"Epona?"

"The Horse Goddess," explained his sister. "And Moon Goddess, too, wasn't she, Father?"

"She was indeed, my dear," agreed the professor. "A Celtic variation of the Greek goddess Artemis – we know her better in the Roman form, as Diana, goddess of the hunt."

"The sacred grove," murmured his daughter almost to herself, "... and the horse, Diana's messenger..."

"The sacred grove?" Purwell was first intrigued, then he chuckled. For once his daughter was confused! "You're getting into a muddle, my dear," he chided her, jokingly. "You're thinking of the legend of the Golden Bough!" Paul joined in his father's gentle laughter, as Diana came out of her momentary waking dream.

"Why did I say that?" she asked, puzzled but smiling,

as her brother took her hand; she knew there was no malice in their amusement.

"Another one of your daydreams," teased Paul. Diana responded with a bright grin.

"Perhaps the Moon Stallion put it into my head!" she laughed, merrily. As their mirth faded, Paul grew thoughtful at the memory of his morning's ride.

"It's a beauty, that stallion." He looked at this sister's blindly attentive face, and teased her again. "Not like that chalk horse at all!"

"You've seen it, Paul," she reminded him. "Please describe it to me." Paul was caught, open-mouthed, and had to admit defeat.

"I don't know how to…"

Purwell straightened from his maps, and moved to a small display case as he spoke. His voice was quietly triumphant, as though hugging a pleasing secret.

"I think I know the answer to that problem," he said gleefully, sliding out a slim tray from the neat rosewood cabinet. The tray contained several antique coins, each one set in an individual well. Very carefully, he took out one worn coin.

"Sir George collects anything and everything to do with horses," he reminded the children, indicating the various ornaments around the room with a gesture of his head. "But this is especially interesting," he said proudly, placing the coin on Diana's open palm.

With the tips of her slender, sensitive fingers, Diana explored the sculptured images on the coin, and a picture formed in her mind's eye. On one side, a head;

but on the obverse, the strangely stylised form of a leaping horse. Minute as it was, its age and quality and life were transmitted as clearly as a vivid melody; and as her father related the dry-as-dust information about the history of the coin, Diana's face grew slowly more radiant with wonder and pleasure.

"It's a Celtic imitation of a gold stater of Philip of Macedon," he explained. "Interesting, the Greek connection. The coin was either imported into early Britain or struck by Belgae settlers here, about the year 100 B.C." Diana hardly heard; she was delighted with the image that her fingertips revealed to her eager mind.

"The White Horse... looks like *this*?" she asked, breathlessly.

"Remarkably similar," said her father, showing the coin briefly to Paul, before replacing it in its tray.

"I still think it looks more like a dragon than a horse," Paul insisted.

Closing the display case, Purwell took his son's arm and urged him towards the map-strewn table. "If that's what you think, my boy," he rummaged about and found the precise map that he needed, "here's something that will interest you!" His finger indicated a particular point on the elaborately sketched contours, and Paul stared closely, trying to read the name written there in spidery, antique script.

"D'you see this, Paul?" The professor tapped the stiff paper enthusiastically. "A tiny natural mound, just below the slope of the chalk horse?" At first Paul could see only a jumble of names and scrawled symbols: tightly dotted rings indicating Uffington Castle, the great earthwork fort cresting White Horse Hill, then, on the dip of the north-facing slope, the tiny symbol marking the White Horse itself. Close by were a series of deep ridges, quaintly named the Manger; and at last, almost trampled beneath the hooves of the chalk horse –

"Dragon Hill!"

"According to local legend, it's where Sir George killed the dragon," explained Purwell, like Paul not noticing the sharp interest in Diana's shadowed face. "Not a single blade of grass has grown on top of the mound since then it's said."

"Why's that?" Paul asked, intrigued.

"The dragon's blood," suggested his father. "Death to all living things, I presume –" He started slightly at Diana's voice, its quiet tone surprisingly incisive.

"But why did it happen beneath *her* sign?"

"What sign?" puzzled Paul. "Whose?"

"Epona's." The name fell from Diana's lips softly, with something close to awe. Her father, matching her meaning, nodded in sombre agreement.

"The Horse Goddess… of course," he murmured.

"And so close to Beltane," continued Diana's quietly insistent voice.

"What are you talking about?" grumbled Paul, irritated that he couldn't follow Diana's line of thought. "You just said Beltane was May the first. St George's Day isn't anywhere…" His voice trailed away. His sister was quite right; a bare eight days separated the two feast days. But what had that got to do with dragon's blood? It was

Purwell who tried to answer his son's question.

"All of the great spring festivals have their roots in violent ritual – St George's Day, Beltane, Easter, the Passover…"

"Sacrifice," the blind girl added.

"To a chalk horse?" declared Paul scornfully. "Whatever next!" Diana either didn't hear, or chose to ignore her brother.

"Father," she said firmly, "I want to go to White Horse Hill myself." She looked towards him, across the shadowed room. "Please take me there." Purwell crossed the room to his daughter, and placed his hands gently on her shoulders. As he spoke, her serious face melted into a smile of expectation.

"We'll take the horse and trap there in the morning," he promised, then added with a chuckle, "but there'll be no dragons, sacrifices or even horse races, I can assure you of that!"

Chapter Five

MORTENHURZE SHADED HIS EYES AGAINST the morning sun and watched the blind girl being helped into the trap by her father. It was only minutes ago that Todman had ridden out with the boy; as they left, the dour stable-master had given his master one last glance, a silent reminder of his earlier demand: keep Purwell and the girl away! But the need to divert Purwell from exploring the chalk horse – if only for a few hours – had now become more urgent. Estelle, hearing of the excursion, had pleaded to be allowed to travel in the trap with Purwell as a companion to Diana, and Mortenhurze could not refuse his daughter's affectionate request. Now they were ready to drive off, with Sam as coachman; unless Mortenhurze acted quickly, Todman's plan to test the boy's suspected powers would be ruined. If the boy *was* a whisperer and could bring the stallion to him, there must be no intruders to prevent Todman from seizing the opportunity. Then, as Sam sat patiently waiting for his master's command to move off, Mortenhurze saw the means by which he could effect a reasonable delay: Purwell's insatiable curiosity about the past.

"Your investigation, Professor," remarked the squire, stepping to the side of the trap closest to Purwell, "where do you plan to start?" He already knew the answer, but the matter had to be broached in a casual fashion, to avoid suspicion.

"The earth fort at Uffington Castle," replied the professor with some surprise, wondering at the question.

"You can see for miles when you reach the top!" Estelle informed Diana excitedly, forgetting those dark, unseeing eyes. Diana smiled, and gave her own reason for the excursion.

"And the White Horse is there," she said.

Mortenhurze glanced at that blind, eager face, then turned affably to look up at Purwell, seated directly over him. "Might I suggest you approach it from the west –" his voice implied a secret advantage to be gained, "– along the Ridgeway?"

Estelle could see no benefit in this, and protested mildly, "That isn't the prettiest route at all, Father."

Mortenhurze glanced at his daughter, and gave her a thin smile. "The professor is neither a poet nor a painter, Estelle," he pointed out drily. "He's an archaeologist."

"Is there something along the Ridgeway I should see?" asked Purwell keenly. Mortenhurze's answer was deliberately casual, but he could see the quickening of interest in Purwell's eyes.

"Wayland's Smithy."

"Of course," murmured the professor, recalling its relative position on the map: little more than a mile from White Horse Hill, and not to be missed.

"What's that, Father?" asked Diana, sensing the excitement in his brief response.

"A megalithic burial chamber, my dear," Purwell informed her, "at least four thousand years old!" Estelle resigned herself to humouring the professor's almost boyish delight, and had to admit the drive up to and along that section of the Ridgeway would be a pleasure on this cloudless May morning.

"It'd be no trouble to look at it on our way, Professor," she suggested, adding thoughtfully, for Diana's sake, "it's in a little grove of trees, off the chalk track. Quite a pretty spot, really."

There was the merest flicker of tension on the blind girl's face as the brief description triggered off an image in her mind's eye... a grove, a sacred place, a place as old as time, its tall trees looming overhead with tendril branches interlocking like fan-vaulting in a cathedral... she could never see it, but she knew she must find it.

"I'd like to go there, Father," she said simply.

*

The creamy chalk track of the Ridgeway gleamed softly in the sunshine, still, deserted and almost silent, as the trap struggled up the last few yards of Odstone Hill to the crossroads formed by the Ridgeway itself and the downland track that reached up, over and across to

Tower Hill beyond. The way up from the lanes below was steep and deeply rutted, a difficult pull. Sam walked at the horse's head, with Purwell, jacketless now, walking at the rear of the trap, and only the girls as passengers. Turning the horse and trap onto the full width of the Ridgeway, Sam eased both to a halt, giving his beast a much-needed breather and the passengers a clear view along the ragged hedgerows of the avenue. Purwell clambered into the trap and sat, his shoes now powdered with fine chalk dust. Breathless and mopping his brow, he smiled at the girls; Diana sat quite still, taking in the countless scents and sounds of this wild, secluded place.

"This is the Ridgeway," Estelle informed the unseeing girl at her side. "It's still used," she added, "by walkers and as a bridle path – but not often."

The journey from Coleshill had been crisp and breathtaking, the trap jinking and weaving along twisting lanes that threaded nimbly through tight-knit hamlets like Shrivenham and Ashbury before turning at last up the steep incline of Odstone Hill. Now at last all was still, all movement frozen like a fly in amber, delicate, precise and timeless. The hedgerows on either side of the broad chalk avenue were already thick with may buds and rambling clusters of wild flowers. Breaks in the hedges gave glimpses of fields and farmland, copses and spinneys edging the uncultivated grasslands with a darker, thrusting green; but in spite of the spacious sweep of open sky, the blanketing silence muffled even the singing of the birds. The travellers relaxed, savouring the tranquil moment, but Diana was aware of something deeper, an undertow, a quality beyond what the others could only see.

"It feels so wild," she murmured, "and very… old."

Purwell, gazing along the empty reaches of the long chalk track, took up Diana's theme.

"Indeed it is," he brooded. "This is one of the three great routes across prehistoric Britain." He turned, slowly scanning the great avenue from east to west. "Joined with the ancient Icknield Way, it stretches all the way from the Wash down to Stonehenge."

"Who made it?" wondered Estelle.

"Iron Age man – as a link between the great earth fortresses he built against invaders."

"Centuries ago," murmured Diana.

"These hills have changed very little since then, I suspect," said the professor. The thought amused Estelle, and she leaned against Diana, smiling into that happy, unseeing face.

"Perhaps Time took a breather, just the way we're doing!" The blind girl's quick smile became thoughtful, as she turned towards her father.

"Or else we've come full circle," she said mysteriously. "Back to where Time started…"

Purwell and Estelle decided that Diana was joking, and laughed pleasantly together. "In that case," Estelle grinned, gesturing to Sam to clamber aboard and take up the reins, "we'd better move on before we're attacked by prehistoric savages!" The two girls giggled at this wild fancy, and bumped together playfully as Sam flicked the reins and walked the horse forward.

Just as Estelle had described it, Wayland's Smithy was set slightly off the Ridgeway, through a lych-gate and along a short path leading into a simple, circular grove of tall trees. Leaving Sam and the trap outside the gate, Purwell and Estelle each took one of Diana's hands and led her forward into the tree-ringed glade. It was cool and shadowed, flecked only here and there by invasions of sunlight through the close-meshed branches tangling overhead. Diana gave a small shiver; not because of the lack of warmth after the bright sunlight of the Ridgeway, but because of what she sensed – the serene but disquieting atmosphere of somewhat sacred. Unable to see, she had no way of explaining; her unease passed unnoticed by her companions, both of whom gazed about, impressed by the glade's simple natural beauty. The trees that formed the ring encircling the grove were tall and stately, and past them, wheat-sown fields could be seen falling gracefully away, with the distant lower slopes of the Vale spread hazily beyond. In the centre of the glade, a long grassy mound was stretched, some six feet high and almost two hundred feet in length, its simplicity broken only at its southernmost tip – the entrance to the chambered barrow inside.

Diana halted abruptly. Her face, blindly uptilted, was unafraid but questioning.

"Are there… stones… at the entrance, Father?" she asked. Both Purwell and Estelle looked at her, intrigued by her moment of intuition.

"Yes, my dear," nodded Purwell, "there are."

"Please show them to me," Diana requested, holding

out the hand she now withdrew from Estelle, to indicate her meaning more clearly. Purwell led her forward without hesitation, used as he was to his daughter's awareness of the unseen. Reaching the massive stones that formed the screened entrance, he took both Diana's hands and placed them gently onto the time-worn surface of the sarsen that silently guarded the tomb doorway, before stepping back, leaving her to pursue her exploration alone. Estelle watched, silent and fascinated by this ritual of introduction; but at Purwell's gesture, moved away, as he did, on a slow wander around the wooded grove.

Diana's fingertips were quite still; they made no attempt to discover the shape or dimensions of the huge, weather-smoothed boulder, but rested lightly on the finely granulated surface as though drawing a deeper knowledge from the very heart of the ancient stone. That knowledge came; a swift, frightening pulse of understanding that could never be put into words, and that both warned and welcomed the blind girl. She gave a small shudder and, withdrawing her fingers from the cold stone, stepped back and stood there, still as the stones themselves. The link was broken and understanding faded into the shadows of her mind. Gathering her senses, she now listened attentively to the movements and voices of her father and Estelle, needing to know they were still with her, that she wasn't alone in this secret, awesome place.

Purwell, walking clockwise around the mound's perimeter, studied it carefully, mentally noting the traditional shape, the small boundary markers set at intervals all around the mound's lowest edge, and the situation of the minute forecourt just behind the guardian stones that screened the innermost opening of the burial chamber itself. He also noted, with a dry smile, that Estelle was bored with the plainness of the place and its gaunt atmosphere.

"It reminds me of going into a church!" she exclaimed brightly, determined to amuse the others. Purwell looked up at the trees spreading their branches overhead and saw the architectural similarity.

"Yes," he agreed, "the trees are like columns beneath a vaulted roof." He had by now arrived full circle by Diana's side, and caught the murmur of her own response.

"Or a wooden temple…"

She was right, Purwell admitted, silently. This place was older by far than even the earliest Christian church, possibly even earlier than Stonehenge and its Neolithic forerunner, Woodhenge. Before that, thousands of years ago, rituals and worship had been practised in natural places related to supernatural power – deep caverns, open hilltops… or wooded glades, just like this one.

"Perhaps you're right, Diana," he said, touching her shoulder fondly. "Time has stood still, here."

Estelle, seeking some sort of physical excitement, ran scrambling onto the top of the mound, and stood there, arms akimbo, king of the castle.

"It doesn't look like a smithy in the least," she complained. "Who *was* Wayland, anyway?"

"An ancient Saxon deity," replied the professor, "the blacksmith of the gods."

"That explains some of the peculiar stories about the place, I suppose," Estelle commented, and Purwell nodded.

"It's said that if you leave your horse and a silver coin beside the capstone, when you return next day the horse will be shod and the coin gone," he informed the girls. Estelle laughed, unimpressed.

"Wayland is supposed to have put horseshoes on the chalk horse, too!" she scoffed. "How ridiculous!" Her peal of laughter as she came running down the side of the mound took Purwell's amused attention from Diana for the moment, and he didn't see the concern that troubled her blind face or hear the contradiction she blurted out, half to herself.

"Not the chalk horse," she corrected, "the *stallion*! For *her*… the Moon Goddess!"

*

To reach the top of White Horse Hill, Todman had ridden to Woolstone Hill and from there cut across the undulating slopes that brought him and Paul to the foot of the earthworks of Uffington Castle. A swift rush and the horses scrambled across the outer ditch and onto the grassy ramparts of the fort. Paul reined in, openly amazed; the view was magnificent. Uncluttered by more than an occasional gorse-bush, the worn, sheep-cropped slopes of the hill fell steeply away, giving an almost uninterrupted view over the Vale and the hills beyond, reaching far into the hazy distance. Paul walked his horse along the grassy rim of the Iron Age fortress, taking in the whole panorama, the immense sweep of downland commanded by this windswept vantage point, and shook his head in admiration.

"Nobody could get *near* here without being seen!" he exclaimed, unaware that Todman was watching him constantly, with a quiet intensity that the boy would have found disturbing, had he noticed.

"Best watchtower for miles," commented the dour stable-master. Paul turned his horse inward, away from the open hills, to view the lawn-like courtyard contained within the high defensive embankments.

"And big enough to hold an army!" Paul guessed, excitedly. Todman surveyed the same ground with less enthusiasm, half an eye on the view beyond.

"They've had fairgrounds and circuses up here before now," he grunted.

"Fairgrounds? Here?"

"Entertainment," explained Todman tersely. "For when they used to scour the White Horse."

"Of course," Paul retorted knowingly, "they had to keep it clear and clean. I suppose the fun and games were provided to keep the workers happy."

"More like a pagan festival, some say."

"What about horse races?" asked Paul eagerly.

"Aye, they had those," came the answer. "Even if men *had* forgotten why." His hooded eyes watched Paul shrewdly, but the boy showed not a flicker of understanding, and Todman dismissed him as a threat. Whatever gift the boy might have, he didn't have self-knowledge – and that was the greatest power of all.

"Where did they race?" Paul called across, and Todman had to curb his irritation at the boy's perpetual questioning. Casually, he walked his horse to the rim of the earthwork bank.

"I'll show you," he said – but reaching the crest, sat on his horse as though turned to stone.

Paul saw, and with a tug of excitement, trotted his horse forward, only to find himself sharply gestured to be still by Todman's warning hand.

"Is it the Moon Stallion?" whispered Paul, leaning forward trying to see. Todman took Paul's bridle and drew his horse on gently. Then, releasing the animal, he pointed slowly and carefully down below.

"There," he muttered quietly. "Below us – to your right!"

Opposite the south face of the earthwork fortress, the valley climbed up onto the flank of Uffington Down, with the startling white track of the Ridgeway running between the two hills, from east to west. Standing there, still and proud, was the Moon Stallion. Once he had caught sight of it, Todman never took his eyes from the creature, but his mind raced. Was the boy a whisperer after all? Had he drawn the stallion to him? Instinctively, Todman rejected this – the signs were all wrong, and in the event it had been Todman himself who had first seen the creature. Yet, there it stood, taunting him... summoned by what strange power? He thrust the question from his mind, letting the need for action guide him. Take the horse now, his senses shouted silently, and ask why it came to you later!

"Are you game to take him, Master Purwell?"

Paul marvelled at the man's icy calm. "Nothing will stop me!" he retorted, tense with suppressed excitement, and with that, gave his horse its head.

The boy's horse was the first to reach the belly of the earth-work moat and start to clamber up and out, but within seconds Todman had passed him and was racing on, straining to reach full gallop. Glancing ahead, he saw the white stallion stand for a moment longer and then break away in an enviably easy gallop towards the Ridgeway and the west. Todman grunted; if the stallion once entered the hedged funnel of the great chalk track, they'd have a clear run at him and more than a chance! But already it was gaining, with an almost careless stride, having the advantage of a downward run, whereas Todman and Paul were forced not only to change direction to their right, but also to cope with the rising ground that would bring them onto the Ridgeway and direct pursuit. Teeth gritted, the stable-master urged his horse forward ruthlessly, and briefly glanced back at the boy trailing yards behind. With a savage gesture, Todman urged him on then looked to his front, past the neck of his own desperately straining mount. His heart leaped. The stallion had made its first mistake, entering the inviting gap in the unkempt hedgerow that swept clean down the length of Woolstone Hill, and setting itself only one avenue of escape – straight ahead along the Ridgeway! Entering that leafy trap, it was for a moment out of sight; in a few strides Todman scrambled his horse onto the gleaming white chalk, and pulled it round to take the same route as the stallion – and in that same moment, it had gone. For as far ahead as Todman could see, the track way was utterly empty. He seethed with bitter frustration. Automatically he had reined the horse back, and now Paul made up lost ground and rode up to Todman. He, too, was amazed and disappointed; it seemed almost beyond belief that the Moon Stallion should vanish from sight so easily.

"We've lost it again!" Paul despaired, but Todman didn't give up so easily.

"Keep riding!" he shouted furiously, his jabbing heels forcing his horse into renewed efforts. "It came this way and it can't escape! Find it!"

Almost as soon as they had entered the high hedgerows of the Ridgeway, they saw the trap, with the figure of Sam standing at the horse's head. It was still a fair distance ahead, but Paul gave a cry of recognition.

"It's Father and Diana! Perhaps they've seen it, too!"

Todman said nothing, but rode steadily on, gripped by a smouldering unease. Mortenhurze had played his part. The trap had been successfully diverted from exploring White Horse Hill; yet the Moon Stallion had come this way, either by accident – or by design. Far ahead, Sam had seen them coming, and waved; it was obvious even at this distance that nothing was wrong there. But if the Moon Stallion hadn't passed this way... *where was it*?

At Wayland's Smithy, Diana was patiently sitting on one of the lower stones at the chamber's entrance. A shadow crossed her face, and she called out, into the shadowy interior, quietly troubled.

"Father – please hurry!"

Purwell emerged, beaming and boyish. "I haven't been inside a burial chamber like this one since –"

He paused, with an air of injured innocence, as Estelle cut in, polite but firm. "Professor," she pointed out, "we shall never see Uffington Castle before lunch if we don't hurry."

"You're right, my dears," he acknowledged. "Forts, not tombs, are the key to Arthur the warrior!"

"Are you sure, Father?" asked Diana gently.

"Oh Diana!" laughed Estelle mischievously. "You'll be telling us that King Arthur's buried here next!"

"Impossible!" snorted Purwell, treating the teasing suggestion as a joke. "Merlin wouldn't have allowed it!" He laughed merrily with Estelle, but Diana was listening keenly to a more distant sound coming from the Ridgeway.

"Horses," she declared, with a small frown.

"It must be Paul and Todman!" cried Estelle, and she ran towards the lych-gate and the chalk track outside. "Let's go and meet them!"

Purwell followed more casually, reluctant to leave Diana completely alone, and arrived at the trap to find a group of serious, questioning faces.

"We were on our way to meet you at White Horse Hill," the professor remarked amiably to his son, but he grew as serious as the others when Paul spoke.

"We saw the Moon Stallion there, Father! And it

came this way!"

"*We've* had no sight of it," mumbled Sam slowly, scratching his tousled head in bafflement.

"Perhaps not," declared Estelle crisply, "but we can help look for it!" She climbed nimbly into the trap, urging Sam to take the reins. "Come on, Sam – this'll make a splendid look-out!"

"It must be around here somewhere!" insisted Paul, but his father shook his head apologetically.

"By all means go ahead and look," he said. "I'll stay here with Diana." Paul nodded, taking the point, and then rode off. Purwell watched them for a moment longer; Estelle standing erect in the trap, steadying herself with a hand on Sam's shoulder, Paul and Todman walking their horses steadily westward, all three vigilant and intent, determined to miss nothing. Purwell shook his head and smiled, then returned to the more intellectual pleasures of the megalithic tomb.

Diana was sitting untroubled and patient as before; she made no comment as her father briefly explained about Paul's latest sighting of the Moon Stallion, but smiled as Purwell fidgeted restlessly at the tomb entrance.

"Aren't you going back to look inside, Father?" she suggested. He was eager to do so, but slightly guilty at leaving her alone.

"Come with me," he said, "let me show you the interior."

Diana shook her head, and folded her hands neatly in her lap. "Go and explore," she commanded gently. "I prefer to sit here in the sunshine."

"You know my weakness for the past too well," Purwell chuckled. He stood and crouched in the stone-framed doorway, about to enter. "I shan't be far," he said, and stepped into the shadows beyond.

It was only moments after her father had left her that Diana suddenly straightened, realising that a shadow had fallen across her hands. She caught her breath and waited. Something so silent in its movement that she had heard nothing now stood between her and the sunlight – but she was not afraid. She was conscious of a quiet, pleasant suspense, a trembling awareness of something majestic and serene close at hand, greeting not threatening. Suddenly she knew, as a velvet muzzle rested softly against her neck and shoulder, the warm breath moist against her skin. Her hands reached up in welcome.

"Moon Stallion!" she whispered, shaking with excitement. She stroked the unseen head slowly and lovingly, her face gently inquisitive. "But why have you come to *me*?"

The answer came as her caress reached up between the stallion's silk-smooth brows. Her hand paused as though halted by some unheard command; in her mind a key turned, a door opened, and an image leapt into vivid life like a star rocket bursting in the night sky.

She was looking, without eyes, at a vision: standing on the crown of that long barrow behind her was the Moon Stallion – but now with a rider on his back, dark and majestic in stark contrast to the moon-glow pallor of the horse. The gleam of armour and an aura of cold glory were only fragments in Diana's mind as the Dark Rider raised one mighty arm in a slow, regal salute. The last thing she saw before oblivion swept her into darkness was that gauntleted, grim hand, pointing past Diana to the distant south.

Chapter Six

PURWELL DUSTED HIS HANDS AS he emerged from the cool, dry darkness of the tomb into the bright sunlight. He blinked, his mind lost in thought as he shielded his eyes against the splintering glare. The cramped inner chambers had been picked clean long ago of any bones or pottery shards that might once have been there; Purwell had soon observed – even in the dim shadows lit only from the door – that others experienced in discovering the past had been there before him. But in spite of the neat, arid interior of the tomb, Purwell was not displeased. In the loose walling that acted as filler between the massive stones of the burial chamber masonry, he had detected small fragments of stone that on closer examination might well give him great personal delight and satisfaction. There was nothing further to be done in the way of major discovery or excavation, but even a tiny flint arrowhead such as the professor now slipped into his pocket might provide an additional if minor insight into the past.

He stepped forward, eager to share his interest with Diana, then stopped short, puzzled. Still half-dazzled by the light, it seemed to Purwell that the glade was utterly deserted. Diana was no longer seated as she had been, on the nearby entrance stone.

"Diana?" he called, wondering if her independent spirit had taken her on an exploration of the trees themselves. A moment later his eyes became accustomed to the change of light; and, looking down, he saw her lying senseless on the ground, partly concealed by the sarsen stones that guarded the tomb. Desperately anxious, he knelt by her side. Unconscious and deathly pale, she was nevertheless breathing steadily and easily; she had fainted, decided Purwell, but help would be needed. He scrambled to his feet and ran towards the lych-gate and the track beyond, calling as he went, "Paul! Estelle! Come quickly!"

The crossroads formed by the Ridgeway and the track descending Odstone Hill was barely half a mile from Wayland's Smithy, and Paul and Estelle were waiting there while Todman obstinately continued the fruitless search for the wild horse. Sam said nothing, baffled by the excitement and confusion, but Estelle saw Paul's gloomy face and made a tentative attempt at cheering him up.

"At least you actually *saw* the Moon Stallion!"

"Catching it's the important thing," Paul complained.

"Only seeing it counts for nothing very much."

Estelle smiled to herself, realising that Diana's brother was nevertheless feeling very pleased with himself; boys liked to keep a tally of their victories.

"That's your third time for far," she said, with mild envy, but her consolation went unheeded; Paul's attention was concentrated on the distant shout drifting towards them on the wind.

"Paul! Where are you?"

Paul wheeled his horse around, his face alert and apprehensive as he recognised his father's voice. "Something's wrong!" he blurted out, and rode off hard along the wide chalk road.

He had reached the gate within minutes and slid hurriedly from the saddle to be greeted by his anxious father. The trap, following swiftly under the urging of Sam's cracking whip, grated to a slithering halt only seconds later. Realising the cause of Purwell's concern, Estelle paused only to drag a rug from the back of the trap, then ran after Paul and his father towards the gate and the wooded glade beyond.

"She may only have fainted," Purwell was explaining as they strode into the clearing, "but if she fell awkwardly…" His words trailed away. There in front of them, holding on to the tallest sarsen for support, stood Diana – still pale, but smiling and unhurt.

"There's nothing wrong, Father," she said reassuringly. "I'm quite all right now."

"Thank heavens for that," exclaimed Purwell fondly, embracing his daughter and insisting that she sat down on the nearest stone, while her brother and Estelle crowded solicitously around her.

"What happened to you?" demanded Paul. Diana didn't answer straight away, but frowned, trying to find words. Estelle settled the rug lightly over the blind girl's shoulders.

"You do look pale," she said. "It doesn't matter about the Moon Stallion – we'll go home now."

"I… saw it," Diana declared quietly. The others stared at her, incredulous and uneasy.

"What?" murmured her father in surprise.

"It… came to me." The blind girl struggled to explain. "I was able to… touch it… feel its breath, its warmth…"

"It was *that* close?" wondered Paul. Estelle was more critical.

"How do you know it was the Moon Stallion?" she questioned. "It might have been *any* horse!"

Paul looked around, noting the surface of the ground about them carefully. "There's no sign of anything here now," he pointed out, "not even a hoof-mark." Purwell looked too, and nodded thoughtfully.

"Are you sure it wasn't just a dream?" Estelle remained unconvinced.

"The stallion was real," Diana insisted. "But I did see something else… inside my head."

"Tell us what you saw," Purwell urged persuasively, taking his daughter's hand. She broke free gently, and stood, carefully orientating herself to face the opening of the chambered barrow; satisfied, she pointed blindly to where she had visualised the Dark Rider.

"The Moon Stallion was up there." She indicated the crown of the barrow. "But there was a rider on his back, in dark armour... and..."

Her voice faltered into stillness. The others stared at the blind girl, held by the strangeness of her mood and the eerie fantasy she had conjured up. It was Todman's arrival in the clearing that eventually broke the tension.

"Anything the matter, miss?" The stable-master had addressed Estelle, but his eyes were on Diana; his jaw tightened at the blind girl's unexpected response.

"You didn't find the Moon Stallion, Mr Todman."

"No, miss," he answered tersely. "It escaped us."

"I know," said Diana softly, but her words were lost as Estelle cheerfully took charge.

"I think we should take Diana home," she declared, and ushered everyone towards the waiting trap.

*

"Whatever happened to the child, sir?" asked Mrs Brookes sympathetically, as she and Purwell stood outside Diana's room after seeing the blind girl comfortably into bed. "Nothing serious, I hope?" It had been years now since Coleshill Hall's housekeeper had been called upon to mother Estelle, or anyone for that matter; but she had been the first to insist that Diana should lie down for the afternoon – and without visitors, what's more. Even the girl's father had been ushered briskly away, but Purwell made no complaint; Mrs Brookes had fed the girl, approved of her appetite, and would defend the child's need for rest to the death, it seemed. Kindly though the housekeeper's concern was, however, the professor was reluctant to explain more than was necessary about the strange, haunting incident that morning. He shook his head in innocent bemusement.

"Nothing more than a moment's dizziness I'd say, Mrs Brookes," he commented casually. "She was alone only for a minute, but she must've just… fainted." Mrs Brookes looked at him knowingly, and nodded.

"Young girls can be like that," she declared confidentially, "especially if they're… delicate."

Purwell gave her a small, polite smile, refusing to be drawn any further; Mrs Brookes wasn't finished with her good-natured enquiries yet, however. "Pity her brother or Miss Estelle hadn't been a bit more companionable," she observed reprovingly. "A blind child shouldn't be left alone like that."

"Diana was with me," explained Purwell. "The others had gone off with Todman – to hunt for the Moon Stallion." Mrs Brookes's reaction to this surprised him.

"That wild horse!" she snapped. "When will they ever learn to leave well alone?" Purwell was suddenly reminded of Diana's unnerving intuition, as the housekeeper went on, aggrievedly, "It's all Todman's fault – it'd all been forgotten about, until he turned up a year ago!"

"Why *is* Sir George so set on taking the stallion?" the professor asked, carefully. "His daughter told Diana something, but it was very confused…"

"She was too young to remember it clearly." Memory saddened the homely face. "M'lady – Lady Mortenhurze that was – went riding alone out over the Downs one fine, clear May-time night. It was a strange, favourite pastime with her." The housekeeper paused, a slight catch in her breath, then went on: "All of a sudden, just as she took the rise of White Horse Hill, there was the Moon Stallion, stood there like a blessed ghost."

"A startling sight," admitted Purwell, "even terrifying –"

"The mistress wasn't afraid, she said." Mrs Brookes shook her head, gently wondering even now. "In fact, she told me afterwards, she'd never seen a creature so fine and commanding." Darkly, she added, "It was as though she *knew*…"

For a moment, Purwell said nothing, but watched the shadowed features of the housekeeper as she nursed her sad, mysterious memories; there was something about her words that was close to Diana's way of thinking and it disturbed him, but he had to know more. "What happened?" he asked softly.

"She was a splendid horsewoman, sir – but her mount shied and threw her, hurt her something cruel." Another brooding pause. "Doctors could do nothing for her. She just wasted away and died – that same midsummer." The simple core of Mortenhurze's tragedy brought back an echo from Purwell's own widowed past. He understood only too well the man's dark sense of loss. As if commenting on the professor's thought, Mrs Brookes picked up the thread.

"The master nearly went out of his mind," she said. "He was in such a rage as I'd never seen before… swore to destroy the stallion, he did." She looked hard at Purwell and wondered if she had said too much, but she saw only sympathy and understanding in his face. Even so, she decided, enough had been said; gripping the tray she had brought from the blind girl's room, the housekeeper started to make her way towards the stairs. "Nine years ago…" she muttered, "… and better left alone!" She paused at Purwell's quietly insistent voice.

"But now he hunts the Moon Stallion again – with Todman as his horse-master. Why?"

"Blind foolishness!" was Mrs Brookes's sharp retort. "Revenge can't bring a body back from the grave!"

*

The smith's hammer rang out and echoed in a brisk, bright rhythm, iron on hot iron, as Josh the farrier put the final shaping to the first horseshoe. Duchess stood patiently close by, her head held soothingly by Sam, but she would give no trouble; Josh's hands were firm and sure, and known to her, and within minutes all four hooves would be safely shod and trimmed. Even though Estelle had seen Josh in action many times before, she watched with almost as much fascination as Paul, seeing it now for the first time. Neither of them noticed the approach of Todman until he was there by their side, his shrewd eyes appraising both horse and farrier and silently approving. The stable-master smiled as Paul's keen interest bubbled into words.

"I wish I could do that!"

"Smithing's a skill and more than a skill, Master Purwell," commented Todman, and his eyes grew thoughtful. "Uncommon men, are blacksmiths."

"Josh is a great character," agreed Estelle, going on to explain to Paul: "He's been shoeing our horses for years."

For once Todman seemed talkative, and his words caught Paul's imagination, as they were meant to. If the boy's trust was to be gained, then here was a carrot to hand. "Smiths've been called healers *and* magicians before now," he said. "Got two Christian saints and untold pagan idols behind 'em, so the tale goes."

"Healers?" grinned Paul, then laughed, cheekily. "I wouldn't let Josh be *my* doctor!"

"Wise lad," chuckled Todman. "They used to be the ones that pulled teeth out at the country fairs!"

Estelle found herself equally intrigued by Todman's titbits of information. "Who were the saints?" she asked him.

"St Clement: he's their patron saint, and his feast day's in November. Fireworks and gunpowder – goes with a real bang, that does. And the other one's St Dunstan; they say he shod the Devil and put Old Nick off of horseshoes for good!"

If Josh heard, he said nothing; his sinewy hands worked quietly on, nailing the second shoe to Duchess's raised hoof, held firm between the farrier's knees.

"Is that why horseshoes are supposed to be lucky?" asked Paul.

"Could be," mused Todman. "Some say there's magic in iron. Then again, some say those two saints are just different names for the heathen gods that brought iron from the skies thousands of years before."

"You're teasing!" laughed Estelle. "Iron isn't magic! And it didn't come from the gods, it has to be dug up from the ground!"

"We know that now miss," retorted the stable-master, "but the first iron man found came from the heavens, didn't it? Comets and shooting stars –"

"Meteors!" added Paul keenly.

"Whatever it was, it looked supernatural," agreed Todman, "so the metal had to be something special, y'see."

"And the men who worked it had to be special, too," said Estelle.

"Masters of fire and metal," nodded the horse-master. "And they knew about horses, too." A glint of arrogance came to his eye as though he secretly included himself in that strange company. "Small wonder men called their like wizards and warlocks – for they'd got a secret power... hadn't they?"

Paul seemed too intent on watching Josh set the third shoe onto Duchess's hoof to hear this last remark, and Estelle was merely amused by how such a comment could possibly apply to the homely farrier working so deftly before them.

"I can't see Josh getting up to any conjuring tricks," she laughed. "He's too busy shoeing horses!"

Todman touched his cap and seemed about to move away, then paused and addressed himself to Paul, casually polite, but commanding the boy's attention.

"Miss Purwell better, is she sir?"

"Yes, she is, thank you," Paul replied, grateful for the

stable-master's interest.

"Delicate sort of girl," continued Todman, drily. "Sensitive."

"I suppose she is... in a way," admitted the boy, reluctantly. Estelle seized on the probable solution with confidence.

"That must be it, Paul," she asserted. "The atmosphere of that place affected her – brought on a sort of daytime nightmare –"

Todman cut in quickly. "Is that what made her faint, d'y'reckon, miss?" he said.

"Diana insisted that the Moon Stallion came to her there, while she was alone." Estelle's disbelief showed clearly; she had no way of knowing the turmoil of Todman's feelings. Paul continued the explanation, equally innocent.

"It happened while we were still searching, apparently."

Shaken and close to anger, Todman could only point out the obvious. "She's blind, isn't she? How *could* she know?" Paul disliked the tone of the stable-master's curt retort, and stared at him coldly.

"She can't explain, but *I* believe her!"

"She says it actually let her stroke its head," Estelle threw in as an aside. Todman stared straight ahead, a cold breath of fear prickling the back of his neck. His voice choked with disbelief.

"She... *touched* it?"

"Then she had this strange dream," Paul said; but before he could recount the vision, Todman exploded in a sharp, sarcastic whisper.

"There's your answer, isn't it? Make-believe! A child, boasting!"

Paul defied him, angrily. "My sister always tells the truth!" he blurted out, fists tight-clenched at his sides. But Todman had already turned away, and Estelle was the first to see why. Striding towards the paddock was her father, clearly, even at this distance, in a rage. The stable-master stood waiting for him, stony-faced; but for her part, Estelle knew that a swift retreat was the simplest way of avoiding the whiplash of her father's tongue.

"Let's go and see if Diana's awake for tea yet!" she cried; and, pulling Paul along with her, ran gaily towards the house. Cheerfully, he took up the challenge and raced her out of sight.

"If you've come to see the gelding...?" Todman calmly questioned his master, knowing this was not the reason for his appearance. Mortenhurze glared at him, totally disregarding the farrier at work.

"I am here to see *you*!" he blazed, quietly.

"You've heard we saw it then," drawled the stable-master, adding as an unnecessary explanation, "the wild horse, I mean."

"The chance was yours and you let it go!" rasped his master. "In God's name, why?"

"There was *no* chance," Todman countered bluntly.

"It was in your grasp, man!"

"We weren't meant to take it – only to see it," retorted Todman. He studied his master's haggard face as his anger subsided into a desperate confusion, and silently pitied the man. "The time wasn't right," he said, "not yet."

"But it came to you while the boy was there!" exclaimed the squire. "Just as you said it would!"

"It isn't him," Todman answered.

There was a small silence. The flush of anger had now drained completely from Mortenhurze's face, and his eyes darkened with a slow dismay. If it wasn't the boy…

"Then she is the rival," he whispered, half to himself. "Purwell's daughter!"

"And her being here is your doing," Todman pointed out coldly and spitefully. Servant was master now, and both knew it, as Todman stared at the squire with a dour, open insolence. Mortenhurze made no attempt at a denial.

"How can I bring her to heel?" he pleaded.

"Through her father," was the curt reply. A small, bitter smile creased the stable-master's sullen mouth. "You're the master here, after all – the professor's patron," he mocked. "If he's to earn his money, let him do as he's told – and keep his blind brat out from under our feet!"

*

Mortenhurze discovered Purwell in the library, immersed in a slim, worn, leather-bound volume – the Reverend Francis Wise's "Letter to Dr Mead concerning some Antiquities in Berkshire", written some hundred and fifty years before. The professor glanced up pleasantly and was about to express his admiration for the Reverend Wise's refreshing powers of observation, when his host's anger burst upon him.

"Purwell!" stormed Mortenhurze, confronting the surprised scholar, "I have commissioned you to investigate a legend that interests us both. I have welcomed your children here as my guests – but they must not be allowed to interfere!" He paused, his voice dropping to a challenging growl. "Or do you find that unreasonable?" Purwell, although taken aback by this sudden verbal onslaught, was not to be browbeaten – least of all over the matter of his children.

"In what way have they hindered my work so far?" he demanded, setting the book aside. "Or are you referring to Diana?"

Mortenhurze was quick to answer. "Because of her, you have spent the day pampering a sick child instead of attending to your investigations, sir!"

"The result of a distraction you yourself suggested," the professor pointed out drily. "Wayland's Smithy."

"That girl of yours is too highly strung!" retorted Mortenhurze. Purwell, determined not to be provoked, remained calm.

"Imaginative, perhaps," he admitted, then added amiably, "but I find that a healthy compensation for her blindness."

"Indeed?" snorted Mortenhurze. "She strokes wild horses that no one else can see, has visions of black knights in shining armour –"

Purwell shrugged aside the scornful tirade. "She builds her excitement on her interest in my work."

"To the point of giving herself nightmares and

fainting fits!"

The jibe went home, and Purwell protested angrily. "That is hardly fair, sir!"

"You'd like a comparison?" Mortenhurze was cold and incisive now. "*My* girl is sensible, rides well and can converse with reasonable intelligence. And she does *not* faint!" Purwell considered this, and smiled.

"They've struck up a charming friendship," he commented. "A pity they can't ride together."

"Out of the question!" snapped Mortenhurze. "Your girl must confine herself to the house and grounds." He allowed himself a touch of bland diplomacy. "For her own peace of mind, there must be no more excursions."

This prohibition was too much for Purwell, and his indignation flared again.

"Diana can travel perfectly well in the trap, as my companion," he declared stiffly. "What's more, I have promised her a visit to the White Horse, and I intend to *keep* that promise!" Mortenhurze misunderstood, and took Purwell aback with the vehemence of his reaction.

"The Moon Stallion is none of your concern, sir!" he exclaimed. "You and your children will keep away from it!" Suddenly Purwell sensed the despair behind his host's anger; he remembered the tragedy that had seared Mortenhurze's life, Mrs Brookes's retelling of the event, and the pain Mortenhurze had shown when Diana recited the saying about the beast of ill omen, and he raised his hands in a gesture of apology and explanation.

"My sole interest is in the *chalk* horse, Sir George," he soothed. "It could play a key part in my investigation.

Does it celebrate Arthur's victory at Mount Badon? Or is it a symbol of some far more ancient purpose?"

"That is for you to establish, of course," responded Mortenhurze, unable to argue with this line of reasoning. "But the girl –"

"An outing on the Downs can do her health nothing but good," insisted the professor gently. "When I proceed there in the morning, I shall take Diana with me." Then, anticipating Sir George's protest, he added quickly, "And having kept that promise, I will continue my research without pause... alone."

*

The two girls sat sunning themselves on the bank above the scoured chalk image of the White Horse. As they listened to the soft, muted sounds of the morning, a skylark rose to challenge the hazy sky above the strangely beaked head of the ancient pictogram; and, looking towards Diana, Estelle touched the blind girl's arm. Diana had already caught the tumble of falling trills and smiled with delight.

"A skylark," she murmured. "I'm not afraid, now." Only minutes before she had been clinging desperately to her father, all sense of balance and solid ground beneath her gone.

"We didn't mean to frighten you," murmured Estelle, still contrite. "We wouldn't've upset you for the world." She let her mind slip back to the tiny incident; accompanying the professor and his children on their morning excursion to Uffington Castle, Estelle had suggested trying out an old local superstition, just for fun. Apparently, to stand in the eye of the White Horse with your eyes closed and turn three times about was lucky – as were white horses and horse shoes, Paul had reminded the girls. Diana had been given the privilege of going first, and leaving Purwell with the horse and trap a little way away, the children had run to the huge ungrassed head and begun the simple ritual. Diana had made a joke about not needing to close her eyes; and, stepping back from her, Paul and Estelle had counted the turns, three times round, to 'bind the spell', laughing merrily. It was then, as she completed that third and final turn, that sheer panic had gripped the blind girl; and, falling to her knees, she had cried out desperately for her father. He had run to her swiftly, as had the two youngsters, and seconds later her feeling of safety had come back to her; but with fear gone, Diana had started asking questions. Would she have fallen? And what was there, far below the slope of the White Horse?

The others had looked – and wondered. The slope fell steeply away to the bare top of Dragon Hill, far below. Paul had recalled its legend, and for a brief moment he had shared something of Diana's fear as he gazed down at the 'killing place', as she had named it, mysteriously. Estelle had seen Diana's unease and drawn her away to safer ground, close by the trap, at the same time urging Purwell and his son to wander off by themselves and explore the earthwork battlements of Uffington Castle. When instead Paul had asked to fly his kite along the hilltop, his father had willingly agreed, in an effort to lighten the tension of the moment. Cheerfully, Purwell had helped the eager boy to collect the kite from the trap, and raced him up the windswept slope until they were out of sight, leaving the girls alone and silent.

"I was safe, anyway, with the White Horse near me," Diana suddenly remarked. "I should've known that."

"You talk about it as though it was a living creature," Estelle frowned. "It's only an image made of chalk."

"It's been here a long time." Diana ran her hand over the cropped grass, thoughtfully. "I think it holds the spirit of the place."

"A ghost, you mean?" puzzled Estelle. Diana shook her head and struggled to explain, but it wasn't easy.

"It's a symbol – a sort of secret message..." She foundered, then exclaimed more brightly, "... like the Moon Stallion!"

"The Moon Stallion is just a wild horse!" Estelle insisted.

"It means more than that to Todman."

"Of course it does!" laughed Estelle. "He wants to train it as a top-class winner! Perhaps *I'll* be able to ride it, one day!"

"No, Estelle!" Diana's response was almost a rebuke. "You must never wish that!"

Estelle stared at the blind, anxious face and frowned. "Why ever not? It's a beauty!"

"Because it represents... something unknown," said Diana softly. Her face had the same strange, lost expression that Estelle had seen before; once when Diana had first recited the Moon Stallion curse, and again when the blind girl had entered the wooded glade that was

Wayland's Smithy. Her brooding voice went on, quietly insistent. "It means something we must never, ever see face to face…"

Before Estelle could question this, Paul and his father made an energetic return over the brow of the grassy embankment. Paul was clearly disappointed.

"It was going well!" he complained bitterly. "Now look what's happened – it's ruined!"

He thrust the box-kite at Estelle with a sullen gesture, and she could see that part of one calico panel had ripped free. Instead of commiserating, she smiled up at him cheerfully, as Purwell arrived and stood by with brisk paternal dignity.

"It's not so bad," she said. "I can mend it for you, if you like, this evening."

"Could you?" Paul was delighted and grinning broadly, dashed off to lay the damaged kite carefully on the seat of the trap. "Thanks!"

Estelle looked across to Purwell as he gazed out at the vast spread of landscape far beyond, his face deep in thought. "Did King Arthur fight the Saxons here, Professor?" she asked. Paul caught her question as he raced back from the trap, and decided to humour his father gently in return for their few minutes' sport with the kite.

"Yes, Father – *is* this Mount Badon?"

"I rather think not," said Purwell with a shake of his head.

"But the White Horse," insisted Paul, "surely that's a monument to Arthur's victory?" It was Diana who answered him.

"Some people claim that it's a monument to King Alfred's greatest victory, as well," she said, "but it can't be."

"Why not?" demanded Estelle.

"Because the chalk horse was first made long before either King Arthur *or* King Alfred," the professor informed the girl kneeling by Diana. "At least a thousand years before."

Paul wasn't convinced; he could see the glory of great battlefields, not of history itself.

"But think how well Arthur's cavalry could attack from up here!" he insisted. His father chuckled quietly at Paul's blinkered enthusiasm.

"Precisely why the Saxons did *not* fight here, my boy!"

"They'd be silly to try," Estelle chimed in, gaily helping to mock Paul's boyish grasp of military strategy. "They'd have no breath left, charging up this hill!" Laughing, she dodged as Paul hurled a handful of grass at her.

"What do girls know about battles?" he protested, and, leaping to his feet, began a jolly, mock-vengeful pursuit of the nimble girl who skipped and scampered out of reach behind the far side of the trap. Purwell, smiling at their playful antics, found his attention drawn back by Diana's quiet comment, directed at him.

"Father, this isn't Mount Badon," she said. Purwell moved close to her side, the other children quite forgotten. He stared at her intently, wondering.

"How can you know that?" he demanded. Her face was calm, full of quiet certainty as she recalled her moment of vision in the wooded glade.

"When I saw the Dark Rider," she said, "he pointed to the south. You must look there."

Chapter Seven

THAT AFTERNOON THE CHILDREN WERE left to amuse themselves. Putting his faith in Diana's intuition, Purwell had taken Mortenhurze into the library immediately after lunch, and over the maps there – and without giving away the source of his inspiration – had proposed Liddington Castle as his next objective. Almost directly south of Coleshill Hall, it was the next major Iron Age fortress due west along the Ridgeway from Uffington, and high on the list of runners as the possible site of Mount Badon. Busily preparing for the afternoon's journey, the professor had said little or nothing of his plans to the children; used to his sudden withdrawals and enthusiasms, they cheerfully accepted Estelle's suggestion to explore the shrubbery and stream beyond the formal perfection of the lawns. Away from the house, amongst the casual tangle of pathways, rhododendrons and towering yew hedges, they would be free of adults and the need to be seen but not heard. Besides, Estelle had promised Paul the chance to try out her new cycling machine, something he'd never ridden before.

Hand in hand with Estelle as her partner, Diana blithely joined in the amusement as Paul's ungainly efforts resulted in yet another tumble.

"He's fallen off again!" laughed Estelle, as Paul struggled to untangle himself from the bicycle's clumsy frame.

"It isn't easy, you know!" he exclaimed good-naturedly, then paused in the process of clambering to his feet; crouching, he gave a small exclamation of distaste. Estelle could just see something on the ground in front of Paul that, to judge by his expression, was strange, or unpleasant, or both. She went to kneel by him, pulling Diana down with her as she, too, gave a small murmur of surprise. Both she and Paul were so engrossed with what they'd found that Diana's ignorance was quite forgotten.

"What is it, Paul?" she demanded. "Please tell me." A large, smooth stone occupied the centre of the clearing; on it was carefully spread a diminutive skeleton. Fragments of coarse skin were the only clue to its identity.

"It looks like a frog... no, a toad," decided Paul. Estelle, studying it over his shoulder, gave a shudder of disagreement.

"*Was* a toad, once, Paul."

"What do you mean?" asked Diana.

"It's dead, and it's horrid," Estelle replied, with a

grimace. Paul edged closer, but held back from touching the little corpse.

"It's been picked almost clean by ants," he observed. Estelle, making weird gestures over it like an Indian princess, grinned and spoke in a deep, mock-ghostly tone.

"It's a sacrifice!" she moaned, then burst out laughing.

Diana's face was serious. "Why do you say that?"

Paul explained, as he always did when Diana needed factual information. "The way it's placed," he told her, "laid out, spread-eagled – it must be deliberate."

"Who'd do a nasty thing like that?" said Estelle, wrinkling her nose at the thought. Paul stood and balanced himself, ready to flick the remains away with his toecap.

"I'll clear it away," he offered, but checked at Diana's warning.

"Someone's coming!"

Estelle, delighted at the chance of an adventure, quickly and quietly ushered her two friends into the cavern-like heart of a nearby rhododendron bush, a den long remembered from earlier tomboy days.

"Let's hide!" she whispered urgently. "In here!"

Hidden, but with a good view past the glossy green leaves, they crouched, still and silent. They held their breath as the approaching footsteps at last reached the clearing and the intruder stood revealed.

Diana breathed her question into Paul's ear, feeling him grow tense with surprise. "Who is it?"

"Todman!" came the almost inaudible reply, and now

Diana shared the silent amazement of her companions. They were barely a safe distance out of earshot, but as Todman knelt before the stone and its macabre offering, he seemed utterly unaware of anything except the puny skeleton and the silent ritual he now performed. His movements were deft, without hesitation, as though he was practised from long experience. Diana could barely contain her curiosity.

"What's he doing?"

"He's found the toad!" murmured Estelle.

"He knew where it was," Paul whispered, his mouth close to Diana's ear, his eyes never leaving Todman for a second. "I think he must've put it there!"

Estelle gave a small gasp. "He's taking its bones!"

"What on earth for?"

Todman had indeed collected every minute fragment of the skeletal form, and now moved to the rippling stream nearby. He knelt there, and raised his lean, brooding face to the sky, his eyes closed as he offered up a prayer. His lips stopped moving, his eyes briefly considered the waters before him – and then with one quick gesture, he scattered the handful of tiny bones onto the bubbling water. Then he leaned forward, watching the bones closely, alert and ready to pounce as they were carried floating and sinking by the trickling stream.

"He's thrown the bones away!" Estelle squeaked breathlessly.

"Where?" asked Diana.

"Into the stream!" responded Paul, then added

quickly, "but he's snatched one of them back – I wonder why?"

Todman held the tiny bone with delicate fingertips and, drying it gently, studied it with a satisfaction close to triumph. Then, abruptly, he stood and walked with quick, lithe strides out of the clearing and through the shrubbery towards the house. For a moment, the children remained in hiding, fascinated by what they had just seen. Suddenly, Diana knew.

"He kept the last bone," she said.

"That's right." Estelle looked puzzled, but was beginning to get used to Diana's moments of understanding, and didn't even bother to ask how Diana had known what she couldn't possibly have seen. "What does it mean?"

"It's the magic bone," the blind girl explained. "What Todman just did – it's a very old and very special ceremony."

Paul looked at her, frowning in disbelief. "Magic?" he exclaimed. "What for?"

"The bone is a talisman – a charm for mastering horses." She paused, and realisation flooded over her face. She turned to the others, excitedly. "It tells us what his name means!" Estelle turned to Paul, completely baffled – just as he was.

"I don't understand what you're talking about, Diana," she muttered. "What about his name?"

"In olden days, horse warlocks used that charm… and they were called 'toadmen'."

"Todman!" her brother blurted out, excitedly.

"But he's already wonderful with horses," Estelle pointed out. "There's nobody better!"

Diana groped her way to a standing position, her face suddenly very serious; their discovery was no longer a childish adventure. "Don't you see?" she demanded. "He needs it for the Moon Stallion!" She struggled to find a path out of the entangling branches, almost desperately. "I must tell Father – before it's too late!"

The trap was already moving briskly away from the house as the children burst out of the bushes along the sweeping driveway in an effort to intercept the professor before he left. Purwell, feeling rather smug at his control over the trotting horse, saw the children; and, thinking they were waving a vigorous goodbye, gave them a cheery wave in return – but didn't stop. He heard Diana's voice calling to him, but he was firm, remembering his promise to Sir George. She would be in good company until his return later in the day.

"Father!" Her cry drifted to him over the sound of wheels and hooves. "Wait...!" She stood quietly dejected, as the trap receded briskly into the distance, her departing father's words thrown back to her in a series of broken but cheerful phrases.

"Off to Liddington... tell you about it later... back this evening..." A longer pause, and then the parting cry, "Goodbye!"

*

The remainder of the afternoon passed pleasantly enough, but as the time slipped away, Diana grew increasingly quiet and more tense. Paul knew the signs of

100

his sister's anxiety, and though he couldn't understand why Purwell's return was so important to Diana's peace of mind, he had gone out to the stable yard more than once to see if their father had returned. His latest enquiry has been made during the early part of the evening; he had come across Todman sorting out horse brasses in the tackroom, and for all his polite concern had been treated as an intruder. The horse-master's abrupt and sullen response had told Paul little more than he already knew, but returning to the drawing room, he had given the girls Todman's answer in more cheerful terms. He found Estelle deftly repairing the torn calico panel on his kite, and hovered at her shoulder, impatient for the sewing to be finished. It took Estelle's reassurance that Liddington wasn't really very far away to remind him of his sister's quiet unease.

"And you know how Father forgets about time when he's interested in a place," Paul added, then frowned in puzzlement at his sister's reply.

"He needn't have gone there."

"But Liddington Castle's an important part of his investigation –"

Diana dismissed this with an insistent shake of her head. "Arthur's battle wasn't *there*!" she asserted, then explained as she sensed the confusion her remark had caused. "Liddington is in the west – the wrong direction altogether."

"You're wrong, Diana," corrected Estelle firmly. "Liddington's south from here."

"It's west of Wayland's Smithy!" the blind girl

retorted, "that's why it's wrong!" She made no attempt to remind them of her vision of the Dark Rider and his eerie salute that was both a greeting and a command, but went on mysteriously, "There's so little time…"

Estelle tried to reassure her. "It's not *that* late, Diana. Father often goes riding much later than this, and I don't worry."

"What is it that's so urgent?" Paul demanded to know.

"Tomorrow's a full moon."

"Yes, it is," agreed Estelle.

"It's also the Celtic feast of Beltane."

Paul tried to joke the growing atmosphere of unease away. "We're not expected to celebrate, are we?" Neither of the girls was amused, and now Estelle was serious as she questioned the blind girl by her side.

"What are you afraid of?" she asked quietly.

"Everything," Diana murmured. "It's such a strange coming together – the full moon… Beltane… the Moon Stallion… Todman and his magic charm…"

Paul looked at her thoughtfully, remembering the leather thong he had seen at Todman's neck not many minutes ago.

"He was wearing it – just now!"

"It's all coincidence!" declared Estelle brightly. "There doesn't *have* to be rhyme or reason, does there?"

"What could possibly happen anyway?"

Diana found it impossible to give her brother the simple answer he demanded; she wasn't even sure herself if the shadow haunting the back of her mind was real or not. "I don't know," she whispered, and gave a little shiver, as though chilled. "But I wish Father would hurry…"

Mrs Brookes had entered the room at Diana's last words, and moved forward, sympathetic but firm.

"He'll be home soon, miss," she comforted, "but it's too late for children to wait up, even so." She indicated the standing clock in the corner, its pendulum quietly swinging the seconds out of sight, and the children knew clearly that the Last Post was being called. "Time enough for questions and answers in the morning. Come along!"

"You're right, Mrs Brookes," admitted Diana. "I'm really very tired."

"Into bed with you then, my dear." The housekeeper cheerfully took the blind girl's arm and drew her to the doorway. "If you're still awake, I daresay your father will look in to say God Bless."

"I'll make sure he does!" declared Paul brightly, holding the door for his sister and Mrs Brookes to leave, and hoping that he would be permitted to remain downstairs a little while longer.

"Sleep well, Diana," called Estelle, implying that she as hostess wasn't ready for bed yet. Mrs Brookes had other ideas, however.

"All of you – no exceptions!" Her manner allowed no refusal and the children went before her, resigned but obedient. "Up the wooden hill." She closed the door on the empty drawing room and the house was still.

*

Alone and brooding in his study, Mortenhurze realised

with a start that the last departing glimmer of daylight had left the room thick with shadows. He was in the process of lighting the oil lamp on his desk when Mrs Brookes knocked and then entered in response to his brusque summons. She stood waiting patiently while the soft glow of the lamp filled the room, and noted without surprise that her master was dressed ready for a night ride.

"There'll be no need for you to wait up, Mrs Brookes," Mortenhurze instructed her.

"But, sir," she protested mildly, "what about Professor Purwell?" She took pride in the fact that her master's guests were always well cared for, and he must know it. "He's not back yet and he'll be famished, poor man."

"If he's any sense at all, he'll have stopped at an inn for the night!"

"We don't know that though, sir, do we?"

"Very well," Mortenhurze conceded. "Leave something for him to eat in the library – but Todman can look after him, when and if he finally arrives."

"I'll make up a cold tray for him, sir… with a decanter?" she enquired discreetly.

"Of course," retorted her master, drily amused that Mrs Brookes guarded his wine cellars almost as carefully as her well stocked pantry. "Are the children in bed?"

"All but one, sir."

The small furrow of irritation on Mortenhurze's forehead eased as Estelle – hiding all the while just outside the study door – stepped inside to deliver an affectionate reprimand to her father. Mrs Brookes slipped quietly away.

"You didn't come to my room to say goodnight."

"So you took the opportunity of coming down," Mortenhurze observed with a dry but fond smile, as Estelle hugged herself close against him.

"Don't I deserve that one small privilege?" She looked up at his lean face, her eyes softly shining in the lamplight. It was as though a memory had come to life, but Mortenhurze thrust the echo from him by firmly acknowledging the reality of the present.

"You are, after all, the lady of the house."

Estelle's response was alert and eager. "Then let me come riding with you!" she begged. "Now, tonight!" Her face fell at her father's curt reply.

"Out of the question."

"I'll be no hindrance – I promise!"

"You know I ride alone at night!" Mortenhurze snapped, and , miserably, Estelle blurted out the reason.

"Ever since nine years ago!" Even as she spoke she knew he was deeply hurt; it hadn't been her intention and she clung to him, desperate for his forgiveness as the pain seeped from him.

"Why of all things must you mention *that*?"

"I'm sorry – truly I am," she whispered. "I didn't mean –"

She looked up at him again, hopefully; he hadn't drawn away. He shook his head, not angry but infinitely sad. "I know," he said.

They clung together, silently sharing the memory of the ghost who had loved them both, so many years ago.

"Mother's death seems so much closer lately," confessed Estelle. Her face was buried against his chest, but she felt him nod; he understood.

"Purwell's daughter…"

Estelle faced him, ready to turn aside his anger, but it didn't come. "She seems to know all the hidden things – but she has no malice, Father!"

"Only a blind honesty." His reply was typically sardonic, but his daughter frowned, sensing a flicker of despair, a secret fear. "A rare but dangerous commodity," he added; then, placing his hands on her shoulders, kissed her gently on the brow and released her.

She smiled and moved to the door slowly and gracefully, her nightgown floating slightly with the movement. He watched her, thankful that she knew nothing of the dark paths that he now trod; but the blind often see more than we find comfortable, he thought, and murmured a last gentle warning to her.

"Do not be led too far by her." She turned at the door and looked back at him. "Goodnight, Estelle."

By a trick of the lamplight, it seemed to the girl that Mortenhurze was almost swallowed by the shadows. Dismissing the thought, she smiled and left him to the night.

Chapter Eight

THE GREAT FRONT DOOR OF the Hall closed with a quietly reverberating thud. Mortenhurze paused on the moonlit steps of the elegant stone portico and, looking out into the night, took in its cool, refreshing fragrance in one long, deep breath. In the distance, an owl exchanged hunting calls with its unseen mate; all was silence, but for the brisk crunch of the squire's boots on the gravel drive as he strode along the looming façade of the hall towards the stable block. A lamp gleamed in the shadowed depths of the library window behind him, a formal welcome for the professor when he returned. Mortenhurze moved on, purposefully. Once in the stable yard, he made his way towards the only other light which challenged the light of the moon, marking his meeting place with Todman: the tackroom.

The stable-master barely troubled to look up from

polishing a crescent horse brass as his master entered, but his quick glance showed him that Mortenhurze was tense and nervous, as well he might be. The squire stood before him, urgent and silently demanding, but still Todman worked on with loving care.

"Are the signs cast yet?"

No reply; only the soft insistent buffing of rag on smooth metal. The horse-master at last flicked a look upward, relishing the growing impatience of his master, and scorning it.

"For God's sake, man – tell me!"

Todman rose to his feet, a thin, triumphant smile on his dour mouth, and gave a curt nod towards a corner of bare earth on the far side of the cluttered tackroom. Mortenhurze moved across to the spot, with Todman a pace behind him at his shoulder.

On the roughly marked out rectangle of naked earth, a handful of gleaming brasses had been thrown down; this was Todman's scrying pit. Where some would read hands, or cards, or even stones, Todman used these randomly scattered horse charms to read the chart of times ahead. At first, Mortenhurze had openly mocked this bizarre method of telling the future. Patiently, Todman had informed him that clairvoyance and the ability to 'see' future time were not tied to the crystal ball and so-called gypsy fortune-tellers. It was an art, practised the world over since remote antiquity. The ancient Greeks had suspended mirrors over running water and seen in them the faces of the dead; medieval diviners had used the highly polished domed lids of copper kettles to reflect images from another world; Arabian scryers would gaze at the bright blade of a naked sword and read the mystic signs they saw beneath the gleaming surface.

Arrogant about his own powers, Todman placed himself above such trance-inducing trickery. His understanding of the ritual horse brasses was in the great secret tradition of Chinese divination – the reading of the random fall of simple bamboo slivers – and followed those dark minds which knew the key to the symbolism of the Tarot cards. In time, Mortenhurze had come to accept and trust Todman's scrying of the brasses as a true guide to the unholy course of action they must pursue, and he mocked no more.

Avidly, Mortenhurze crouched to study the signs, but it was Todman who gave their pattern meaning.

"Here's tonight's full moon..." he indicated a full, shining disc of brass, then pointed to a crescent shape further away, "... and this crescent is the Moon Goddess." He shifted his position to indicate the next sign, an open hand. "And here *you* are, master – the Taking Hand, or Hunter as some call it." There was a wildness in his eyes as he explained the significance of the signs. He pointed out yet another brass – this one a horse rearing. "And *here*," his voice dropped to a whisper, "is the horse, our prize – the Moon Stallion! See how it's touched both by the land and the crescent – a perfect unity!"

"It couldn't be better!" exclaimed Mortenhurze.

"Three throws I've made," declared the horse-master, with satisfaction, "and always the horse is hobbled." He grinned full into Mortenhurze's face. "You can't fail... master."

The squire, his mind filled only with dreams of future triumph, ignored the casual insolence, and rose to his full height, arrogant and determined. "It's moonrise now," he said. "Time to ride out."

"And by dawn the stallion'll be yours." As Todman spoke, he knelt and took up the scattered brasses from the scrying pit. Apart from those he had just read, there were several turned face down and of no importance. But one brass, barely enclosed by the uppermost boundary of the rectangle, caught the eye of Mortenhurze. Its position had not apparently merited Todman's attention, but it was nevertheless strangely dominant, and the squire bent to look more closely at its symbol: a spoked wheel.

"The Wheel," he queried, "what does it mean?"

Todman picked up the brass and considered it carefully as it lay in the palm of his calloused hand.

"Some call it Fate," came his reply, "but others call it the sign of the Traveller."

A picture of the professor driving off to Liddington came into Mortenhurze's mind, and he frowned. "Purwell...? Can *he* interfere?"

"Look where he was," indicated Todman. "Lost – right outside the event." He set down the handful of brasses on a nearby shelf, ready for the next scrying session. "Don't worry, he'll not bother us."

Reassured by Todman's confidence, Mortenhurze nodded. Then, without speaking, they walked to the nearby stall where Rollo stood saddled and ready for the midnight ride. Todman went to the beast, and soothing him with murmured words, led him out into the yard where Mortenhurze stood waiting, taut as a bowstring. Seconds later he was effortlessly in the saddle and waiting for the next stage of the ritual that would send him on his way.

Todman now stood at the horse's shoulder; he took the leather thong from around his neck and held it up for Mortenhurze to see. From his hand dangled the pale, slender piece of bone; but close to it, part of the same potent charm, was a silver crescent, gleaming as it twisted, slowly spinning in the moonlight. For one still moment the two men stared, captivated by the frail talisman; then Mortenhurze took it, slowly clenching it in his fist, savouring the power it represented. Todman watched his master's face with dark, strangely impassive eyes, then gave a quiet order.

"No time to lose, master." Mortenhurze came back to reality, fastening the talisman to the horse's bridle, as Todman continued, "You know where you ride?"

"To White Horse Hill."

"Take the high ground there – and keep close watch."

"Until dawn, if needs be," Mortenhurze said eagerly.

"The Beltane fire."

Todman's eyes glinted up at Mortenhurze, dark commanding pools in a moon-pale face. His voice was low, quietly emphatic.

"A fire not made by man... but it will be there, somewhere on those hills..."

Mortenhurze nodded; his mind raced, recalling the

countless times Todman had told the legend of dark capture. The power of the magic fire would draw the Moon Stallion to it, make it captive, hold it helpless; the talisman would do the rest… and their triumph would be complete.

"It'll be yours for the taking," said Todman, as though reading his master's thoughts, "for you have the moon charm."

Mortenhurze leaned over his horse's neck, stroking it, and then reached for the talisman. He held it in his fingers, a brooding excitement in his voice. "And the words of power?" he said.

"Zabaoth – Firiel – Samantas!" Todman chanted hypnotically. "Use them and you cannot be denied!"

Mortenhurze straightened in the saddle, arrogantly. "When I return –" he began, but it was Todman who completed the prediction.

"We will share that moment, master. I will have the power I seek… and you will have revenge!"

He stepped back from the horse, and touched his forehead in a farewell salute. Rollo moved forward at his master's touch, and in a slow, parade-ground walk, left the yard. A cold, calculating smile shadowed Todman's lips as he watched horse and rider reached the gravelled driveway, break into a canter and melt from sight into the silvered stretch of parkland and beyond. At last even the soft thud of hoofbeats on the turf faded into silence. Turning on his heel, the stable-master walked back towards the tackroom. The night would be long, but he dared not sleep; a vigil must be kept, and before midnight there needed to be another casting of the signs in the scrying pit.

It was many years ago now since the signs had begun to lead him here to Coleshill; years of subterfuge and sly persuasion, years of servility, of holding his scorn and pride in check, years of scrying and dark calculations before this one night, the keystone of the year numbered nine, when his ambitions could be achieved. If they failed now, everything was lost; it would be another nine times nine before the omens met in perfect unity again.

Todman stopped short of the tackroom and frowned, not at the thought of failure, but at the approaching sound of a horse and trap, travelling even now over the gravel of the sweeping driveway. He turned in time to see the shadowy vehicle cautiously enter the stable yard and move slowly towards him. It halted, and for a moment he couldn't see beyond the flickering gleam of the side lamps, but he knew the driver must be the professor. Stepping forward, Todman held the horse, gently comforting the beast, his hand on its neck, as Purwell descended stiff-legged from the trap.

"Home at last, Todman!" he exclaimed with a tired smile, grateful to be on his feet once more and no longer at the mercy of the unseen ruts and potholes of night-shaded country lanes.

"You didn't stay overnight at Liddington after all, sir," blandly commented Todman, his mind counting up one more omen in his favour. Safely home, there was no way the professor could be an obstacle to Mortenhurze's plans; the portent of the Wheel in the scrying pit could be discounted, as Todman had foreseen. He listened amiably, as Purwell explained his lateness.

"Lost myself on the way back, as it happens."

"Not difficult, in these old lanes, sir."

The professor chuckled as he collected the Gladstone bag that held some of his equipment. "True, Todman – but it's an ill wind eh?" Todman looked suitably puzzled, and the horse blew, as though equally mystified.

"Sir?" queried the stable-master, politely.

"I may have lost my way back," Purwell crowed, "but in doing so, I've found *the answer*!" The professor moved into the lamplight and Todman saw the shine of boyish delight revive the tired eyes. "It was there, staring me in the face!"

"What was, sir?"

"*Baydon*, man! It actually exists!"

Todman almost burst out laughing at the man's childishness, his foolish enthusiasm over such a trivial fragment of useless information. So much learning and so little real knowledge: what earthly use were the long-dead names and dates of history, compared to the powers of nature outside time, waiting only to be unlocked by the hand of one who *knew*?

"That'll please the master, I dare say," Todman commented indifferently, silently amused. Even if he did know, Mortenhurze wouldn't give a damn for precious King Arthur at this moment – he had a far greater glory to pursue! He saw that Purwell had at last gathered up his things, ready to make his way towards the house.

"I must tell Sir George immediately," insisted the

professor. "Where will I find him, d'you know, Todman?"

"The master's out on a night ride, sir," came the dampening reply. Purwell paused for a moment, put out.

"Pity," he muttered. "It will have to wait until the morning, I suppose." He began walking again, less vigorously. Behind his back, Todman smirked.

"There's food and wine set out for you in the library, sir," he called out after the professor, who gave a wave of acknowledgement, pleased at the thought.

"Excellent!" responded the tired archaeologist, and left Todman to tend and unharness the horse.

*

The food set out by Mrs Brookes was little less than a feast, and Purwell had done full justice to it. He hadn't wasted his time while eating, however; spread out beside the tray was the map. Sipping the last of the wine in his glass, the professor stared with dry satisfaction at the symbols and contours marked in black and white that now had so much more meaning. He chuckled to himself gleefully, and drained the glass, then sat bolt upright, suddenly alert. The door had opened, and a figure stood there silhouetted against the light from the passageway outside.

"Sir George?" Purwell peered hard, to see who it was. The figure stepped forward into the glow of the solitary lamp; it was Paul.

"It's me, Father," he said, rumpled and drowsy-eyed.

"My dear boy," smiled his father in greeting, "you should be in bed and asleep!"

"I had to see if you were back." Paul glanced with hungry curiosity at the last remaining slivers of cold ham. His father noticed, and pushed the nearly empty plate towards the boy for him to pick at what was left. "What happened to keep you so late?" Paul asked, through a mouthful of delicious meat. Purwell studied his son, and glowed with good-natured smugness.

"I took a wrong turning –" he confessed cheerfully, "– and made an exciting discovery!"

Paul helped himself to the last tiny fragments, but his eyes were eagerly on his father. "Something you found at Liddington Castle?" Purwell shook his head, eyes twinkling, holding his secret to himself until the last moment, gleefully. Paul could see it was going to be a guessing game, and decided it was worth it if it meant staying up even later. "*Was* it the site of Arthur's battle?" he guessed. Another denial from his father.

"I am certain it was *not*."

"What then?" asked Paul, conceding defeat as he finished the last of the cheese. "I give up!"

Purwell leaned across the table into the brightness of the lamp; his face was a picture of delight and triumph. "I have discovered the real Baydon!"

"It exists after all?" wondered his son, then looked to where his father was pointing on the map, his finger urgent with excitement. He indicated one particular road, running for most of its length as straight as an arrow to the north-west, from Newbury; close to Liddington it changed direction fractionally, but then, straight as ever, sped over the sprawl of Swindon directly towards Cirencester. To the east of Liddington, where this elegant Roman avenue crossed the highest ridges of the downs above Aldbourne, a small village straddled the road before it swooped down into the valley of the Wanborough Plain.

"This tiny village?" asked Paul.

"Baydon," confirmed his father. "There is only a minor variation in the name – and more important, it fulfils all the necessary conditions!"

Paul studied the spot carefully; did it fit the bill as Father claimed? "Set on high ground," he mused, but was then interrupted by Purwell showing other, related landmarks.

"Here, just two miles away, is Membury Fort! Massive earthwork defences – Iron Age, most likely – but screened by trees, giving horse troops far better cover than either Liddington *or* Uffington!"

"This road Baydon's on," continued Paul, after noting his father's point, "it's a Roman road –"

"The Ermin Way, so called," agreed Purwell eagerly.

"The Saxons were bound to travel along it – it's ideal for foot soldiers or wagons."

"And for an ambush!" the professor claimed. "Cavalry sweeping in from positions hidden either at Liddington or Membury, to join battle at 'Mount' Baydon!" He chuckled, gleefully. "I must've been blind to it before!"

Paul didn't seem to hear. Intent on studying the map, he drew his father's attention to where Baydon was marked, and then to a point directly above it, to the north.

"Father," he remarked with some surprise, "Baydon is directly south of Wayland's Smithy."

Purwell threw a sharp glance at his son, then bent forward over the map. Paul was right – but more important, Diana had known it even before her father had driven off to Liddington. Father and son stared at each other, wonderingly.

"Diana said... the Dark Rider pointed to the south," Purwell murmured. "But he pointed from Wayland's Smithy – not from here where we stand!"

"She said you'd gone to the wrong place – she tried to stop you, but it was too late." Paul pulled a wry face. "And *we* thought it was only a dream!"

"I believe her," said Purwell, "but I should've thought it out more logically."

"You did find the place, though;" insisted his son, then added pointedly, "and if Diana was right about Baydon..." He frowned as his father sank back into his chair, brooding and thoughtful, "Father – who... or what... is the Dark Rider?"

"A figment of Diana's imagination," the professor replied briskly, trying to be casual, when in fact his mind was a whirlpool of seething questions. "The physical embodiment of her intuition if you like – an illusion produced by too much excited discussion about Arthur and his legends."

"But her dream came true!" insisted Paul.

Purwell looked at his son quizzically, then gave a smile that pushed the mystery aside. "Then we must tell her so," he said.

"Now?" said Paul, surprised and delighted at the fun of it.

"We stand in Arthur's footsteps, my boy!" chuckled the professor. "That news is too good to keep to ourselves!"

Without more ado, he took Paul by the arm and drew him out of the library and up the stairs to Diana's room. Quietly, so as not to disturb the rest of the household, they tiptoed to her door and opened it with infinite caution. Purwell had brought the library table lamp with him to light the way, and now he held it high as he stood just inside the door, casting its soft illumination into the room and sending the shadows scuttling into the farthest corners.

Paul stood at his father's shoulder, peering in, eager to be the first to wake his sister – but Purwell's rigid arm checked his movement. The smile on the professor's face turned to an expression of dismay; the bed had been slept in, but was now empty. Diana was gone.

Chapter Nine

IT WASN'T THE MOONLIGHT FALLING across the pillow and onto Diana's face that had awakened her; although her blind eyes opened and she saw nothing, it was her whole being that had come alert in answer to a strange, silent summons. Almost immediately on coming to bed, she had fallen into a tranquil, dreamless sleep. Then, as the moon that she could never see started its slow march across the night sky outside her window, a soft, insistent voice had called her, wordlessly, as though from some deep, distant chamber of her mind.

Instinctively, her body made its protest; her face tensed, turning into the pillow, seeking escape. One hand, resting outside the coverlet, clenched tightly as if warding off some unknown fear. Her soft, languid breathing became, for one brief moment of panic, abrupt and desperate. Almost in the same instant, she found peace. The tension within her sleeping body slipped away in one long, gentle sigh; her unseeing eyes opened. She knew that whoever or whatever summoned her held no terror – only a protecting wisdom close to love. Calmly, she sat upright in one swift movement, listening, fully awake now.

Slipping from beneath the bedclothes, she stood barefooted and perfectly still beside the bed, judging her position. Then, quietly and with serene assurance, she moved towards the window and the moonlight that spilled onto the carpeted floor. At the window she paused again, a white slender figure, her ankle-length nightgown flowing in shimmering folds, stark against the room's shadows behind her. Face uptilted eagerly, she looked upward with blind eyes at the full moon riding the night sky and smiled in response to the silvery caress she could sense but couldn't see; and in that smile there was a brightness close to jubilation as, again, that silent, silvery voice summoned her out into the night.

Diana turned and walked to the door. Feeling for the glazed doorknob with delicate caution, she opened the door and stood without moving, listening intently to the murmur of distant voices drifting up the stairwell from a room below. One was brusque and commanding, the other warmer, more concerned, a woman's voice. Someone younger and brighter now joined in, and the blind girl knew it was Estelle. A door closed, burying the continuing conversation behind a barrier of solid mahogany. A woman's footsteps moved briskly, fading into another deeper part of the house, and moments later all was still.

Diana stepped onto the landing and closed her own door without a sound. She knew she must go and could picture in her mind the route she needed to take to escape the house; she had no need of eyes. She reached for and found the polished stair-rail, and, on naked feet, moved silently down to the cool tiles of the hallway below. From here she glided through the shadows of slumbering passageways until she reached the half-glassed door that led first into the conservatory, then through its humid fragrance out onto the garden terraces beyond. The night air was cool and fresh, but Diana was untroubled. She moved across the worn flagstones of the terrace to the balustrade that overlooked the ornamental lawns and flowerbeds, shadowed and eerie in the pallid moonlight, and stood there, blindly seeking what she knew must be there: the Moon Stallion.

Again that silent command, guiding her; and now her calmly searching face was still, looking with unseeing eyes across the silvery lawns towards the looming darkness of the shrubbery. Silhouetted there, like the moon against the night sky, was the Moon Stallion. As her senses located the horse, the eerie creature first lowered, then boldly tossed its ghostly head, in a silent welcome and salute. There was no need to answer; Diana stepped gracefully down the broad terraced stairway and, without hesitation, crossed the wide lawn to the midnight meeting. Reaching the stallion's side, she was met by the gleaming muzzle dipping into her raised hand, and with a smile of complete trust she laid her cheek against the velvet-skinned muscles of that mighty shoulder. The silent greeting over, the stallion moved gently away, drawing the blind girl with it to the tree stump of a once-towering elm. At first confused, Diana quickly felt and identified the gnarled bole and, from its near-flat upper surface, realised its purpose – it was a stepping block to mount the horse. Within moments she was on its back and they had merged as one, the fingers of the blind girl lacing into the thickly rippling mane, her own hair flowing as freely as her moonlit gown. Her breathless apprehension melted into pleasure as, with a slow thrust of power, the ghostly stallion walked majestically into the shadows of the shrubbery. A dozen strides later, with garden and house now far behind, they were galloping across parkland into the night wind.

*

The ride, without vision, was a flight into darkness but not fear. The sear of the wind, the rushing of the stallion's hooves, the pounding and relentless surge beneath her blended with the secret sounds of the earth set free by the tides of the moon, sweeping Diana into the very heart of night. Time no longer had meaning; earth and air merged, hill and valley melted into one unceasing, rhythmic stride, and the blind girl laughed into the wind, knowing what it was to ride Pegasus, winged stallion of the gods. Diana, her body rippling in unison with the motion of the horse, felt a sudden stab of dismay as the pace slackened first to a canter, then to a walk; the journey mustn't end now! She wanted it to last for ever! Then her disappointment was overridden by a new excitement, an understanding that this journey was only a beginning. Where the Moon Stallion was taking her she couldn't tell, but her elation grew with every stride. At last the stallion stood stock still. Diana hardly dared to breathe, knowing that they had reached their destination, that this was journey's end. She slipped down from the stallion's back, and waited.

*

The moon-dappled trees loomed over the blind girl like a midnight cathedral; all unknowing, she stood before sarsens half as old as time itself, the stallion still as a statue by her side. But the tomb the stones guarded was no longer dead. From deep inside the burial chamber, a glow of pulsing, sinuously shifting light flared softly out, fingering girl and horse, sarsen and tree trunk, with its amber bale-fire. Touched by the light, sensing something of its warmth, Diana put out a tentative hand, unafraid but questioning. As though in answer, a deep, vibrant, ancient voice seeped echoing from the tomb – and hearing it, Diana reached out to the stallion at her side for reassurance.

"Diana, child of the Moon!" The words were both a salutation and command. "Answer!"

"Where am I?" she demanded bravely.

"The stones will tell you," came a voice again. "Question them!"

Diana stepped forward slowly, both hands out-stretched, and in a few paces reached the sarsen stone guarding the ancient tomb. As her fingertips examined the time-worn granulations of the rock, her blind face grew bright with understanding and she cried out aloud.

"Wayland's Smithy!"

"I am here," called the voice, deep within the tomb. "Come to me, Moon Child."

Grim and commanding though the voice was, Diana sensed it held no threat for her; guided by fingers and bare feet, she edged her way into the tiny, stone-flagged forecourt, and entered the tomb.

Without flame or smoke, its blaze not kindled by man, the bale-fire filled the innermost heart of the burial chamber with an eerie, pulsating radiance. Outlined in its grow was a burly, hunched figure; the helmet on his head was horned, his close-wrapped cloak caught at the shoulder by a huge, jewelled clasp, his brooding, bearded face forever shadowed. Diana entered cautiously and stood quite still but unafraid. Her eyes glinted, bright but sightless, in a sudden flare of the fire. An awareness of something immensely ancient, wise beyond time and sad beyond understanding, prompted her to kneel – not from fear, but with awe and the deep respect that a pupil might have for a teacher of great wisdom and experience. The bale-fire cast on her neither heat nor chill, and she knew she was free to question what she could not see.

"Are you Wayland?" she asked gently.

"I have been given that name, among others." The cloaked shoulders shrugged, infinitely weary. "Some have called me Volund; some have hailed me as the Green King; some, perhaps, have known me as Merlin…" The rasping whisper trailed away. Diana's mouth dropped open in amazement at the last name.

BRIAN HAYLES

"Merlin?"

"Master of iron... and magic." A note of pride crept into his voice. "Master, too, of these hills – named Odstone, after the metal they once held... empty hills, now." The figure hunched deeper into his cloak.

"The lodestone!" Diana's face brightened as the meaning fell into place. "There was iron here once!"

"Iron that made man the arbiter of life and death," the voice rasped sadly, then paused before continuing, with a sharper edge of bitterness. "Yours is the new Iron Age."

Diana remembered her father's academic distrust of Science and Industry and their dark, satanic progress.

"You mean the Age of Science," she corrected.

"One name and many names," retorted the Green King. "The magic of ancient times forgotten, in darkness, now rediscovered... and not understanding its past, rushing forward only to find self-destruction as so many times before..."

"Yet you remain."

"Guardian of a power that only sleeps... awaiting its reawakening."

A prickle of apprehension ran through Diana; there was a key here, a link between her father and Mortenhurze, an unopened door that led to something dark and dangerous.

"Like Arthur, the Dark Rider," she said. "What were you to him?"

The Green King straightened, his voice proud. "I was Arthur's counsellor and priest. I was servant to Epona, the Moon Goddess. I was blacksmith and magician – who else could have forged the magic sword, Excalibur?"

"*And* shod the Moon Stallion?"

A dry chuckle preceded his answer. "That, too… but before that, and forever afterward, I guard the power and mysteries of this ancient place, sacred to the goddess known to me as Epona, to the Greek as Artemis –"

"– to the Romans as Diana of the Woods!"

"One name and many…" The ancient voice grew soft at some remembered vision. As though chanting a ritual incantation to bind the listening girl with the age-long thread, the Green King spoke slowly, his words resounding through the chamber. "The moon is her chariot. She rules the tides of Fate, the Wheel of Being…" He paused, as if inviting the girl to continue the liturgy, and the voice Diana heard next was her own.

"The Moon Stallion is her messenger –"

"– and the White Horse on the hill, her alter-sign and omen."

The bale-fire flared as the Green King completed the calling of Epona, but no sound disturbed the stillness of the night. Diana raised her face to the guardian of the grove. She knew now his part in the legends of the goddess – but what was hers?

"Why am I called to you?" she asked.

"You are her namesake, and protected," came the reply. "No one can see my face and live!"

"Yet you need me?"

"You have a part to play."

"What must I do?"

There was a pause; then a rustle of movement told Diana that the Green King had drawn closer to her. She remained kneeling and motionless, waiting to do what she must, without question. But when the voice of the unseen being spoke again, softly and almost at her ear, it held the blind girl spellbound. In it she sensed desperation born of centuries of suffering, and her throat grew tight with sympathy.

"Take what I offer you," the voice demanded, "without fear!"

Diana reached out towards him, but his pain was almost too much to bear, and for a fraction of a second her hand hovered, trembling. In an agonised whisper, he drove her on.

"Moon Child – obey!" commanded the Green King. "Give me a new life and the power to do what must be done! Release me from the bonds of Time!"

Her fingers closed around what she found, and returned once more to her lap, grasping a small, leafed burden. The Green King gave a low murmur of relief, and drew back.

Instinctively, Diana's fingers began to examine what she now held. It was a sprig from a plant, firm yet supple; at one end of the miniature stake there was a point where the shaft had been torn from its parent body, and at the other grew leaves and a tiny clutch of smooth round berries. She couldn't see the leaves and bark coloured like antique gold, or the seed-bearing fruit gleaming milk-silver – but suddenly she knew both what it was and its ancient, sacred meaning.

"Mistletoe!" she exclaimed softly. "The Golden Bough!"

Memories of knowledge gleaned from her father reminded Diana of the plant that grew seemingly by magic, not from soil but from the limbs of the living oak, itself a sacred tree; a golden, secret plant, revered both by the priests of ancient Greece and the Druids, magic-masters of the Celts; a plant known more tragically in Nordic legend as the innocent stake used to pierce the heart of Baldur, the once-eternal god of light. There was an elemental mystery here, and Beltane was only part of it.

"Life upon life," responded the Green King as though answering Diana's thought, "but also the death-bringer…" The blind girl's mind danced with shadows and the words she spoke were theirs, not her own.

"That is the Wheel of Being," she echoed, "constantly turning full circle, never at rest."

"Life, death and life again," responded the Green King, "these are the seasons of mankind…" From the shadowed depths of that majestic cloak, a great gauntleted hand reached out in an imperious yet soothing gesture that commanded those unseeing eyes to close. "Open your inner eye, and behold – the Wheel turns!"

The arm and gauntlet were gnarled and mossy, like the bark of an immensely aged tree, but Diana was no longer aware of the Green King; her face tilted upward, radiant with wonderment, lost in a kaleidoscopic vision that was to take her centuries ahead through time.

*

The images poured through her mind like a torrent, slowly at first, but dragging Diana relentlessly towards understanding. There was no pause for thought or explanation; only events and people, buildings and machines, tumbling briefly into place then just as quickly swept away, to be instantly replaced by fragments of a world that the blind girl soon came to realise had no recognisable connection with her own. All the while there was a deeper undercurrent of fear, lurking and insidious, a threat of a threat that at last openly declared itself as the grim theme of this turbulent vision: man's perpetual quest for a power which, once gained, disintegrated into dust and ashes.

At first the images seemed to form a majestic parade of the greatest wonders of man's history: the huge megalithic gateway at Mycenae, the mighty stone circles of Stonehenge, the lofty temples of ancient Egypt, dominated by towering statues of its god-like kings; but every image had its counterpart of ruin and destruction. A faceless statue of a pharaoh gazed blindly out across the barren desert that once had been his glorious empire; the perfectly cast bronze of a famous Greek hero was lost in an image of the crumbling temple of Athena; a Roman emperor gestured commandingly from a proud stallion, capturing the victories of war in marble, but overshadowed by the ruins of that amphitheatre of blood, the Coliseum; the soaring magnificence of a medieval cathedral was blurred by images of princely machines of war, blasting into ruin a once-impregnable castle tower.

The richness and elegance of ornate palaces of the eighteenth century, a sweeping terrace of gleaming houses, grew dark and vanished beneath a dazzling climax of achievement in the great iron and glass structure that had testified to the skills of engineer and craftsman half a century before: Crystal Palace, showcase for the Victorian Empire.

But now the mood changed. Diana saw horse-drawn guns hopelessly bogged down in mud and craters, and the emergence of a new invincible – the mighty Dreadnought armoured tank, the epitome of mechanical brutality. Now a tall-towered city graced the shores of Manhattan; an immense, man-made dam held back the waters of the Colorado Valley, a source of vital power; overhead, a strange new menace rode the skies – an airship, proud, graceful and deceptively innocent. In contrast, saddening images of the horse, now no more than a toy – proud stallions dancing like puppets in a school of dressage, feather-bedecked ponies 'cantering endlessly around a circus ring, racehorses walking past the betting boards. The full tyranny of the machine now began to tell; racing cars, their massive engines making the drivers look like dwarfs, sleek bird-machines racing against the skies, but, most cruel of all, the reminder of the machine's finest hour: WAR.

Helpless, Diana could only watch as the grim parade swept by – machines carrying men, guns and more machines across shattered battlefields; machines from beneath the sea that destroyed machines floating on the sea; flying machines that droned and screamed across the smoke-filled skies to hurl destruction onto the already savaged land below; great clamouring temples of industry where machines made more machines that in turn made war.

Suddenly, a strange idyllic scene of peace – a field of ripe corn rippling beneath sun and wind, but that image, too, destroyed by the inexorable march of mighty machines that devoured the harvest, processed it and packed it in great hallways where human hands were simply slaves to automated commerce.

Now came the coda of achievement and destruction, engines that were, to Diana, meaningless in shape and form, but carried a death-dealing power that verged on the god-like. The images flicked by, even faster, moving towards an end that now became inevitable: the stately ascent of an immense rocket thrusting its challenge into space; a silent, mechanical insect, slowly circling the earth, its antennae seeking and finding its distant prey; without the mercy of a human hand to grant reprieve, the doomsday holocaust – a stupefying ball of fire topped by the swollen mushroom cloud that marked Armageddon.

Diana was numbed by that obliterating terror, but still the relentless stream of images flowed through her mind. Now a bleak, barren landscape, scorched by unearthly fire, dominated the vision – a city in ruins, refugees shambling through shattered streets, their vehicles, machines and engines broken and immobile. Sleek trains stood silent in vast, empty railway stations; huge vessels lay rusting on sullen tides lapping deserted harbours; machines without flight sprawled, crumpled like broken wings, on wind-haunted airfields; a solitary car stood slewed across a lonely country road... but still there was life.

Far from the machine-made motorways, the refugees stumbled through the blighted land, trekking across the open fields and moorlands, frail human beings fleeing from a bitter past, seeking a new future, a thin, straggling line of hope. As though on pilgrimage, they walked the road beneath the great White Horse; and there on its topmost ridge, silhouetted starkly against the cruel sky, stood a lone sentinel astride a proud white stallion. This was the final image; as it lingered, fading into the shadows of her mind, Diana knew and understood.

"The Dark Rider," she whispered, "the once and future king!"

*

It was over, and darkness returned behind her eyes; but with it came exhilaration, and Diana faced the Green King calmly, without despair.

"An end and a new beginning..." murmured the blind child, the shaft of mistletoe still between her fingers, a golden talisman.

"Man reaches out to the stars," proclaimed the being framed by the Beltane fire, "and destroying his roots, turns the Wheel full circle to complete his own destruction. Only the Force that has been there always remains to guide him back to his renewal."

"Why did you let me see?" Diana asked.

"It is your right, Moon Child, for you are a part of

that dream." The brooding whisper took on a sterner edge. "But even with your knowledge, you cannot change what you have seen. Accept – and be at peace."

Diana nodded, but frowned as she remembered Mortenhurze and Todman; in some way, they too were linked with man's unending lust for power, but what was her part in their dark adventure?

"Why was I summoned to release you?" she asked the grim shadow before her.

"There are enemies," came the cold response.

"But what is it they want?"

"One seeks destruction. He will find it." The Green King's voice was quiet, but it sent a chill down Diana's spine as he continued, "The other seeks power beyond the right of man. He will meet it."

The blind girl sensed the challenge that his words implied, and knew that Mortenhurze and Todman were more than casual intruders. "They're... very close," she said.

"Do not fear them, Moon Child," said the Green King. "What you are and what you hold protects you."

Instinctively Diana held the spray of berried mistletoe more tightly in her fingers; she could not see the dying flicker of the bale-fire sink into deeper shadow, as in the gathering darkness the last eerie whisper of farewell reached her from the priest-king of the sacred grove.

"Their coming means danger... but only for a while..."

Diana stood, dismissed – and then turned sharply in alarm, hearing the quiet, urgent whinny of the Moon

Stallion. It was both a warning and a challenge, and as quickly as she could she fumbled her way outside to stand, white-gowned and ghostly, at the entrance to the tomb. Her young voice rang out bravely.

"Who is there?"

The answer was a shout of wild defiance.

"Mortenhurze!"

Chapter Ten

COLESHILL HALL HAD SOON BEEN left behind by Rollo's swift stride. Mortenhurze had taken the most direct route he knew, riding down into the Vale between Longcot and Watchfield before skirting the darkened windows of Woolstone village to the east. Now, almost immediately ahead, his midnight destination loomed against the moonlit sky: White Horse Hill. How many times he had ridden these dark hills before, he thought, as he took the lower, undulating slopes of the Manger; but never with the burning certainty he now felt. He remembered those earlier night rides, vengeful and desperate, of nine years ago; he had hunted the Moon Stallion first in anger, later in despair, and always in ignorance. Blinded by his sorrow, he had used only the way of the hunter to run his unearthly quarry down; but this was not enough. Not until Todman had brought his subtle skills and offered them to Mortenhurze had the squire understood how and when the quest could be achieved. From that point on, he had placed himself in the hands of the gypsy horse-master, as an eager accomplice. He knew only too well the scorn with which Todman regarded his tragic obsession, but a bargain had been struck. Until the white stallion was taken, Todman's quiet insolence must be swallowed whole, his presence tolerated. Wait until it is done, Mortenhurze told himself – we will see who is the master then!

Reaching the uppermost slopes, he walked his horse to the crest of the earthwork fortress; from here he could see every hill, every moonlit landmark, the merest glimmer of window-light or fire for miles around. This was the watchtower; and, hawk-eyed and unmoving, Mortenhurze stared grimly out into the night, seeking one certain sign, to be seen only on this one May night: the secret, magical fire of Beltane. Rollo blew quietly into the still, silvered air, but like his master was otherwise as poised and silent as a bronze-cast statue. Mortenhurze hardly seemed to breathe; his head and eyes moved only fractionally as he scanned the nightscape all around him. Cold concentration blotted out every unwanted sound, every unnecessary distraction; nothing else existed in the world.

Suddenly, it was there. A distant, flickering glow pulsed fitfully behind the far-off trees along the Ridgeway to the west, and Mortenhurze exclaimed, loud in spite of himself: "The Beltane fire!"

He blinked hard to clear his straining eyes, but his

certainty was confirmed with a second, longer stare; from its position, it could be nothing else! His heart pumping with elation, he urged Rollo down the moonlit slopes and rode towards the Ridgeway.

*

A bare half a mile along the pale chalk track, Mortenhurze reined his horse back to a gentle walk. Now the glow of the fire could be seen only occasionally between gaps in the shadowed hedgerows, but he knew where it must be centred – at Wayland's Smithy! He frowned, wondering why it should be so, but a moment later dismissed the thought as unimportant. Wherever it burned, the bale-fire must draw the stallion to it – and once there, it would meet a new master! Coming to the break that gave access to the wooded glade, he brought Rollo to a halt and slipped cautiously from the saddle. Looping his horse's rein onto the gate post, Mortenhurze stared into the heart of the clump of trees. At first he could only see the bale-fire glow throbbing eerily from the depth of the sarsen-guarded tomb, but as he looked again, his eyes probing the moon-flecked shadows of the glade, he tensed with sudden excitement, his unease forgotten.

Standing beside the burial mound was the Moon Stallion, gleaming white and motionless.

Mortenhurze swallowed hard, his mouth dry. Without taking his eyes from the wondrous horse, he felt for and released the charm loosely caught on Rollo's bridle. It came free easily and rested in his hand; and, clenching his fist about the toad bone and crescent, he mentally rehearsed the words of power. The time for using them had come and the stallion was within his grasp; calmly, with a feeling of complete command, he stepped forward into the glade, and, raising his arm, dangled the moon charm high, letting its bone and silver forms gleam and glitter in the cool moonlight. The stallion made no move; it seemed transfixed, and when at last it gave an anxious whinny, Mortenhurze almost laughed at the power he held over the wild beast.

In that same moment, his heart leapt with fear; breath and time were frozen into a terrifying stillness. Out of the heart of the Beltane fire, stepping onto the capstone of the tomb, came a white-gowned figure which, in that eerie place, seemed like the spirit of the moon itself… *and it spoke.*

"Who is there?"

"Mortenhurze!" came the desperate reply, his defiance only a veneer concealing terror and dismay. But there was a blind obstinacy in Mortenhurze's stand, too. The moment was his to take; there could be no going back now!

"Give me the Moon Stallion!" he shouted.

"It is not mine to give." The voice was crystal-clear, commanding, but strangely gentle. "Leave this place… before it is too late!"

Mortenhurze faltered; then his obsession and the moon charm gave him greater courage, and he thrust the talisman before him, defiantly.

"I have the words of power!"

Diana's warning came too late to prevent

Mortenhurze from starting his dark incantation.

"In the name of Zabaoth…" The rest was never to be spoken. With a great shrieking whinny, the moon-dappled stallion by Diana's side lunged forward like a white demon to rear high over Mortenhurze, lashing down at him with silvered hooves. Rooted to the spot, Mortenhurze sank to one knee and cowered beneath the stallion's fury; it reared again, and as he instinctively threw up an arm to protect his head from those terrifying blows, the talisman spun from his nerveless fingers into the shadows. His face contorted with fear, he grovelled desperately to regain the charm that was his only hope of safety, but it was forever lost to him. All protection gone, Mortenhurze could only cringe closer to the ground, his fear-crooked fingers scrabbling and clawing as he tried desperately to crawl out of range. Then, for the third time, the Moon Stallion reared high and gave that awe-inspiring neigh; and from the stillness of the night, retribution came.

Out of nowhere, a shrieking storm wind sprang as if from the very heart of heaven, plucking at Mortenhurze like a giant's hand and hurling him to the ground again with the force of an explosion, blinding all his senses with its sound and fury. He caught only one brief glimpse of the Moon Stallion, now calm and still, beside that motionless figure at the entrance to the tomb – and saw with dismay close to panic that they were utterly untouched by the wind that lashed only him, the intruder. Not a hair moved on the stallion's mane, not a fold of the moon child's gown rippled in that unearthly wind – and hearing yet another sound above that tormented howl, Mortenhurze lurched to his feet, his face wild with terror. For what he heard, mingling with the demon voices of the air, was the ominous, dreaded sound of unearthly hooves galloping out of the night sky, a savage stampede of unseen horsemen relentlessly seeking out their quarry: Mortenhurze.

He turned, and, driven by the fearful wind, stumbled desperately from the glade; but there was no escape. He gave one last mournful cry of terror and ran.

"The Wild Hunt!" His voice echoed and was lost amongst the ageless trees. "God help me, Todman – I am lost!" With a superhuman effort he tore himself free of the ravening fingers of the wind, and blundered like a crippled, hunted animal out of the sacred grove and onto the open Ridgeway. Behind him, the white figure stood alone now in that silent place…

Mortenhurze ran. Wild-eyed and gasping for breath, he flailed his way along the white, relentless track that gave no refuge from the hounds of vengeance that pursued him. Haggard, already close to the limits of exhaustion, he ripped away the cravat from his throat, desperate for air, his chest panting and heaving, his throat dry with terror. Through the fear that gripped him came only one clear thought: to run, past pain, past endurance, until his heart burst.

His lagging feet caught on a clump of coarse grass and he staggered, straining desperately to keep his balance, his speed, his impetus, towards the safety that must lie before him, however far ahead; but unseen hands clutched at his ankles and he fell, scoring knees and knuckles raw, his muscles contracting with pain. He lay on the cool white chalk, his breath baying in his throat, and felt an aching desire for peace throb through his body. He needed only to sleep, to find oblivion, to let this hungry wind flow over him and carry the pain, the incredible pain, away…

But there could be no rest. The demon wind plucked at him, urging him onwards; the Wild Hunt knew no mercy – he must flee! Lurching to his feet, he swayed, almost drunk with exhaustion, but instinct commanded his legs to act, and from sheer terror the limbs obeyed. Somehow he ran on, clumsy with ungainly panic, the hideous pursuit so close its savage drumming pounded inside his very skull. Somehow he found new energy, in a last, desperate attempt to escape the crushing thunder of those dreaded hooves; mocked by the cruel demons of the wind, he hurled them from him with flailing arms, and, gulping great sobs of air, still managed to make a race of it – a race against death, a race for survival, a race that in the running would honour *her*… Epona. Shadows and fantasies scudded across his mind like clouds across the moon. As he ran, tongue lolling, the only hunt he knew was there behind him, scarlet-jacketed, fronted by baying hounds, and he the fox.

The shadows cleared for a moment as sweat stung his eyes and he wiped his brow clear upon his sleeve. Forcing himself to see clearly what was ahead, he realised that he had left the broad ribbon of the Ridgeway; it lay faintly glimmering in the dying moonlight far behind him now. The ground came up to meet him, and he saw that he was on a grassy bank, the far side of the earthen moat that bounded the crest of White Horse Hill. His spirit leapt with a moment's hope – there was sanctuary here! Scrambling and clawing his way upward, he came at last to the upper rim and paused there, panting for breath. Still no peace, still the Wild Hunt thundered at him out of the vast night sky. With a choked, incoherent moan, Mortenhurze staggered on, obeying the instinct that told him he must reach the north slope and *her* sign... and at last he stood there, teetering against the skyline, a shattered hulk, begging for mercy.

There was none. Behind him, the sound of those relentless hooves; below him, darkness and the ghostly blur of something white, an apron of hope, peace perhaps... Dragon Hill. He looked back, eyes wild and widening, as across the open hilltop came the gleaming leader of that vengeful hunt – the Moon Stallion. Mortenhurze turned away, eyes tightly closed, all pride gone. Spreading his arms wide as if in supplication, he stepped forward into darkness, and in that moment, knew that he had been betrayed...

*

The moon was down. The tomb, now dark and lifeless, held no sign of bale-fire and only Diana stood at the sarsen stone, her blind face sad and tragic. She gave a small shiver; the night was past, and with it, a life. The elation and the mystery gone, she felt cold stone beneath her naked feet and knew she must leave this place. She stepped forward onto dewy grass and walked carefully on, not yet knowing where her feet would take her. Suddenly a sharpness beneath her toes made her stop. She crouched, and, kneeling, fumbled for the tiny obstacle. Finding it, her fingers told her what it was – a leather thong, and on it a tiny bone tied as companion to a smooth metallic crescent: Todman's talisman. She held it for a moment, brooding over it; it had done Mortenhurze only harm. Then she understood that its purpose wasn't yet fulfilled, and standing, placed it over her head and around her slender neck. As though responding to the subtle power of the charm, a horse whinnied gently from nearby. Diana listened carefully, and guided by its second call, moved blindly but confidently towards the tethered animal. Reaching him, she found his head and stroked it, sadly: Rollo had no master now. Using the barred gate, she mounted the horse and softly commanded him to take her home.

Chapter Eleven

THEY HAD SEARCHED THE WHOLE house; Diana was nowhere to be found. Studying the anxious faces looking to him for leadership, Purwell stood before the reviving fire in the drawing room and tried to piece together the facts so far. Like Paul and Estelle, Mrs Brookes was closely wrapped in a dressing-gown; she had been the first person the professor had alerted, for she knew best the labyrinth of rooms that spread through the great house. Disturbed by the whispering bustle and confusion, Estelle had quickly joined the search party, eagerly scouting those hidden corners that only children know; but there was no trace of the blind girl anywhere.

"What could've happened to the child?" murmured Mrs Brookes, voicing the question in all their minds.

"There were no signs of a struggle." Burglary or abduction seemed unthinkable, but Purwell forced himself to consider the possibilities. Paul, restless and frustrated at having no lead to follow, nodded keenly.

"Then she must've gone of her own free will," he decided. Estelle remained mystified.

"But why?" she demanded, almost angrily. "Where would she go?"

There seemed to be no answers, only the simple fact that Diana had left her bed and vanished from the house completely. Purwell felt helpless, uncertain which course to take; he was not a natural leader, and this kind of incident needed, more than anything else, a man of action.

"If only Mortenhurze was here!" he exclaimed. Estelle looked up sharply, her tired eyes flicking towards the marble clock upon the mantelpiece, and she frowned; in less than two hours it would be dawn. Silently, she questioned the housekeeper standing by her side, and in spite of the warm, reassuring response, felt a qualm of unease.

"The master's stayed out until sunrise before now, miss," Mrs Brookes pointed out. "He's sure to be back soon." Estelle smiled brightly, determined to shake off the feeling of gloom. She stood, ready to renew the search with cheerful enthusiasm.

"We must split up into two groups this time," she suggested. "Diana's probably lost herself in the house, looking for you, Professor!"

Paul nodded in agreement. "She *was* worried about you being so late, Father," he said; then, reminding his father of their own midnight meeting in the library when

Paul had come down to see whether Purwell had returned, he added, "We both were."

Irritated by his own helplessness and by the thought
that he might himself be the unwitting cause of his
daughter's disappearance, Purwell snapped back.

"Haven't we already looked?" he demanded. "She
could hardly go far – and why doesn't she answer to our
calls?" His toughness wasn't eased by Mrs Brookes'
innocent attempt at being helpful.

"Sleepwalking, was she, sir?"

"She has never done so before, Mrs Brookes!" the
professor retorted, but listened more thoughtfully as
Estelle reinforced Paul's earlier suggestion.

"Her mind was very troubled," she insisted. "She was
desperate to talk to you before you left for Liddington."

"Troubled? About what?"

Estelle threw a sharp glance at Paul, wondering how
much she should say about Diana's fears of Todman and
the talisman. It was obvious from Paul's face that he too
was at a loss for a convincing explanation. "Oh…
coincidences," she said lamely.

"The stallion," Paul offered. Purwell noticed the
housekeeper give a small frown as the boy went on, "And
then there was the full moon, and Beltane –" he looked
to his father, hoping for understanding. "You know how
Diana's mind works."

Purwell understood only too well. He recalled the
incident at Wayland's Smithy less than two days ago –
Diana's vision of the Dark Rider, her moment of
unnerving clairvoyance, the visitation by the wild white

147

horse – and from past experience, he knew that the girl would never draw back when confronted by a mystery, she would only go on…

"Perhaps you're right after all, Mrs Brookes," the professor conceded reluctantly, to Paul's astonishment.

"Diana – sleepwalking?" He sprang to his absent sister's defence firmly. "No, Father!"

"Not that exactly, Paul," Purwell struggled to explain, "but somehow living out this new obsession… in a waking nightmare, perhaps?" He turned to his son, and a look of understanding passed between them. Paul had been keen enough to hunt the wild horse; why shouldn't his sister do the same, in her own mysterious fashion?

"She's never gone out to look for the Moon Stallion!" the boy exclaimed. "At night – and alone?"

There was a small silence. The idea had a disturbing logic; it made sense. Each of the four people in the room had his own notion of the Moon Stallion: to Mrs Brookes, it was a dark superstition to be avoided at all costs; to Paul, a gleaming prize to be taken bravely; to Purwell, an intriguing mystery nagging at the mind; to Estelle, a confusion of sad memory and her father's burning ambition to have it for his own; but they all knew that Paul's alarming suggestion spelled only danger for the blind girl.

"She could be anywhere out there…" murmured Estelle, looking out past the uncurtained windows to the dark hills beyond. Purwell was suddenly decisive.

"Get dressed," he told the children, assuming quite rightly that they would help without question, then explained his intention. "We will need horses."

*

They had scrambled into suitable clothing and hurried to the stable yard within minutes, leaving Mrs Brookes to explain their absence to Mortenhurze on his return. But at the stables they met an unexpected and infuriating obstacle – Todman. He listened impassively while the professor told him what had happened, and his stern face gave away nothing of what was in his mind, although it was already seething with questions. At midnight he had scried the brasses, and from their cast he knew something was desperately wrong: that although Mortenhurze had played his part, the final challenge was yet to be faced.

Now Purwell brought him news of the blind girl, and an echo of his unease on first meeting her from the train returned. Always she stood like a pale shadow in his path, frail, sightless and innocent, like a secret omen. A suspicion rankled in Todman's mind; unable physically to intervene, this slender rival might well choose to sow panic and confusion with a pretence at being 'lost'. His resolve strengthened; the blind girl's plan must not succeed – these fools had to be kept from Mortenhurze until the ritual was complete. His mind refocused on Purwell's concluding plea.

"She could be anywhere between here and White Horse Hill!"

"Run away?" The dour stable-master probed Purwell for the truth. "Or taken?"

"Sleepwalking," admitted the professor reluctantly.

"A nightmare trance."

"Then we've no way of knowing where she is, sir."

"Using horses, we can find her!" insisted Paul.

Todman stared at the youngster coldly, putting him in his place. "Not without my master's say-so."

"*I say* so!" flared Estelle. "You've got *my* permission!"

"I don't answer to you, miss... not in this." The stable-master chose his words carefully. "Proper authority – nothing less'll do."

"How is that possible, man?" Purwell demanded angrily. "Sir George hasn't yet returned.

"Then we must wait," said Todman calmly.

Purwell, seeing that anger wouldn't move the stable-master, softened his tone. "A blind girl walking barefoot through the night – have you *no* compassion?"

"No, sir... not without my master's word."

Estelle made to speak furiously again, but Todman looked at her sternly. "Tell me, miss – would your father thank me for risking horse or rider in this poor light?" She shook her head miserably. Only an expert rider dared ride out before daybreak in these hills; at least there was only about another hour before sun-up. Todman nodded, as though reading her mind.

"Be patient, miss," he said, then looked up at the sky shrewdly. "By the time we've saddled horses, it'll be dawn – and your father'll be here to guide us." He alone knew that Mortenhurze would never return alive, but the lie had to be maintained, at least until sunrise.

Purwell stepped back, resigned to having to watch Todman's preparations; Paul was sullen, and moved impatiently towards the stalls, still closed. But Todman was not to be hurried, and he paused as Estelle threw an anxious glance at Rollo's empty stall.

"He's always come back by now," she murmured.

"No need to worry, miss."

"An accident *can* happen!"

"Not to a rider of quality," countered Todman, and turned towards the inner stable, ready to select the best mounts. Paul was already there, shouting irritably.

"Can't we hurry? Diana could be hurt!"

Todman was not listening. He had checked his turn, and stood staring at the gateway to the half-lit stable yard. Puzzled, the others looked at him, then followed the line of his astonished gaze – and were themselves amazed. Entering the gateway was Rollo, with Diana as her rider. The horse stopped, reins loose upon his neck, without command. The blind girl was very still, sensing her journey was at an end; her fingers held the sprig of mistletoe, and round her neck, half-hidden by her flowing hair, was the talisman. Her nightgown, pallid against the brightening dawn sky, made it seem for one split second as though Rollo was carrying a ghost. When she called out, gently questioning, the voice was real enough, and Purwell and his son rushed forward to welcome her.

"Father? Are you there?"

"Thank God you're safe," was all he could mutter into her night-fragrant hair, and drew her down from the horse's back into a close, tight-knit embrace that enfolded all three of them in warm reunion.

Behind them, Estelle and Todman stood fast, disturbed at recognising the horse that had brought Diana home. Rooted to the spot, Estelle felt a wave of quiet dismay sweep over her; fighting her fear, she watched Todman move to take Rollo by the bridle. His expression confirmed what she already knew. Todman stood at Rollo's neck, hiding the turmoil of questions in his mind in fussing the proud, tired beast. He glanced at the blind girl, as the family trio opened their embrace to include Estelle, who still held back. The stable-master barely had time to notice the talisman hanging as a pendant at Diana's throat before she could move past him, stepping towards the sound of Estelle's desperate question, her face tired but strangely calm.

"What has happened?" Estelle's voice was only a whisper, but its edge made Purwell and his son suddenly aware of her fear. Diana moved closer, not answering; Estelle met her half way, and taking her hand, spoke again, trying to be brave.

"That's Rollo, Father's horse –"

"Yes," said Diana, simply.

Mounting panic threatened to drown Estelle's eyes in tears, but she stiffened, her hands gripping Diana's fingers ever more tightly, as Todman's harsh voice rang out across the yard.

"How did you ride it here?"

Diana didn't even glance at him as she replied, all her attention on the girl beside her. "It brought me," she answered. Todman seemed determined to ask more, but was curtly waved away by Purwell as he moved towards the two girls. Diana gently drew Estelle close, resting her free arm around those trembling shoulders.

"Dearest Estelle," she murmured softly, "be brave." There was warmth but also a command in her voice, and the girl didn't break; instead they stood together in silent communion, giving and taking a secret strength. Paul, not fully understanding, saw that his father was deeply moved; and, following his example, hung back.

Purwell's emotions were strangely mixed; he had realised that Diana was in some way the bearer of tragic news, and sensed what it must be – but he had also seen the fragment of mistletoe in his daughter's hand as it rested on Estelle's hunched shoulder, and was silently amazed. How had she come by it? There was no way that she could have plucked it herself, yet in her hand she held an antique wand, like those used more than two thousand years ago in the cult of the Golden Bough… His instant of reverie was broken by Estelle drawing back from Diana's shoulder to question that blind face.

"Tell me what has happened to Father," she insisted, with quiet self-control. Diana frowned.

"I can't… not properly," she said.

Todman strode forward abruptly, drawing the horse with him. His eyes were wild, demanding answers, the truth. "You have the master's horse!" he rasped. "Tell us how you came by it!"

Still Diana didn't reply, and now her father stepped close to her side, urging her to answer. "Diana, we have to know," he said gently.

She turned slowly to face the distant hills from where

Rollo had brought her. Towards the east, the barely risen sun tinged the scattered clouds with a cruel fire-glow. Diana's face was sad as she told the others what they had to know.

"You'll find him on Dragon Hill," she whispered.

*

Mortenhurze was sprawled face down upon the barren chalk where Diana had told them – on the mound beneath the image of the great White Horse. Sam drove the trap that carried Purwell and Estelle, while Todman travelled as outrider on a separate mount. Paul had stayed behind with his sister, now safely in bed and under the care of Mrs Brookes. Purwell knelt by the stiff, spread-eagled body, indicating that Estelle should stay back while he examined it. For what seemed like an eternity, he checked pulse and respiration, desperately hoping for a remnant of life, as Estelle watched, controlled and rigid. Close by, Todman was at hand in case of need, his face a wooden mask, his eyes flicking over the hillside to find some sign, however strange, to explain what had happened. On the road below the mound, the trap stood waiting, with Sam hunched in the seat, giving the group an occasional glance of puzzled curiosity. Why had they come all this way to look at the top of Dragon Hill?

He quickly knew. Purwell stood, grim-faced, then moved to Estelle to tell her the cold truth. She said nothing. He made a gesture of sympathy, but drew back, realising it would do no good. She watched, straight-backed and defiant in the face of grief, as Todman helped

Purwell carry the corpse down to the trap, there to be covered by a rug, while Sam sat staring desperately to his front, wide-eyed and dry-lipped at the thought that his trap was now a hearse and the body in it that of his master. Soon they were ready to go, and Purwell looked up at the crest of Dragon Hill where Estelle still stood, cloaked and unmoving, wrapped in a private world of sadness. Silhouetted against the sky, her gaze was not directed at the body waiting to be taken home; instead, she looked higher, to the cruel image that marked the place of death, an echo of Diana's words spinning inside her shadowed mind. The blind girl had called it the 'killing place'…

*

The death of Mortenhurze, once officially established, took over Coleshill Hall and transformed both the house and all those living in it. The symbols of grief and bereavement would soon be everywhere; already, barely an hour after her return from Dragon Hill, Estelle was dressed in mourning black, with her hair combed from its normally exuberant ringlets into a severe, more grown-up style. Her young face seemed older, more mature, and seated with Purwell in the drawing room, she was his equal, completely in command both of herself and of her new estate. Purwell, watching the child closely for any signs of strain, saw instead a young woman, a daughter Mortenhurze would have been proud of, quietly autocratic, mistress of her affairs as she calmly instructed Mrs Brookes on what must be done.

"You will put the house into mourning, Mrs

Brookes."

"It's already in hand, Miss," responded the housekeeper gently, knowing that soon the tears must come. She found herself being quietly reproved, and Purwell hid a dry smile as Estelle made her new position quite clear.

"Thank you, Mrs Brookes, but the responsibility is mine from now on."

"If there is anything *I* can do...?" offered the professor amiably, only to find that he too was given short shrift, in spite of his good intentions.

"Nothing, thank you," came the pleasant but cool response. "It is a family affair."

"But the funeral formalities –" Purwell started to point out, but found himself checked again.

"I shall need advice," admitted Estelle, then making a small, gracious gesture towards the housekeeper, "but Mrs Brookes will guide me."

Purwell, realising that he was no longer dealing with a child, gave Estelle an encouraging smile. "Of course," he admitted, "you are the lady of the house now."

The phrase – echoing her father's last words to her before his fateful night ride – made Estelle straighten and clench her hands tightly, fighting the impulse to weep hot tears. Another breath and she was herself again, but Mrs Brookes had seen. Catching Purwell's eye, the housekeeper gave a small, sad smile, but his attention was drawn back to Estelle.

"You're welcome to stay until the funeral, Professor," she said, "– if you don't think it'll upset Paul and Diana too much?"

"They'd be only too happy," he nodded. "Young friends in the house might help."

"But your investigation is over. There's no point now... is there?"

Purwell started in surprise; this was something he hadn't expected. Instinctively, he defended his position. "It was your father's dream!" he argued. "My latest discoveries must be pursued –"

Her cool voice cut him short, politely. "But not here." She stood, dismissing him. "My father is dead, and so is Arthur. Let it rest at that."

Chapter Twelve

"CAN'T YOU REMEMBER ANYTHING AT all?" asked Paul. Diana had slept for most of the morning, with her brother sitting at the bedside eagerly waiting for the chance to question her. She had woken hungry and refreshed; the late breakfast brought by Mrs Brookes was quickly eaten, the tray removed, and now brother and sister were alone. Paul wanted answers, but they were slow in coming.

Diana frowned reluctantly, and Paul decided to try and jog her memory. He picked up the strange talisman from where it rested beside the sprig of mistletoe on the bedside table. He studied the tiny bone and the silver crescent for a moment, then lowered them gently into his sister's open hand. As he spoke, her fingers clenched upon the charm and recognised it.

"You were wearing this," he told her, "when you came

back."

"It was his," murmured Diana, remembering with a small shiver. "A very special charm…"

"For protection?" She nodded, and Paul went on, puzzled. "Against what?"

The polished silver was cool against Diana's slender fingers as she tried to put its meaning into words. "Some people fear the power of the moon; some seek that power for their own…"

"But what's that got to do with Mortenhurze?" Paul demanded. "It was Todman who made the toad-bone charm – we saw him!"

"It was Mortenhurze who tried to steal the Moon Stallion," said Diana. Paul stared at her, wondering.

"Is that what killed him?"

"He failed… because he didn't understand the danger." Her face grew sad with the dark memory, and Paul leaned forward, eager to know more.

"You *do* know what happened to Mortenhurze!" he exclaimed. Diana held up the charm by its leather thong, and it slowly untwisted, spinning hypnotically as she answered.

"He was the Beltane sacrifice."

Paul stared at the charm, troubled; a slow anger was growing in his mind. "If it was made specially for Mortenhurze… then Todman must've known!" He stood, suddenly determined, and moved to the door. "I'm going to ask him point blank."

"Paul – you must be cleverer than that –" Diana gestured him to wait "– or he won't tell you anything!"

Paul took the point, reluctantly, but he wasn't going to be put off entirely. "I can talk to him, can't I?" He turned to go, and bumped into his father.

"Where are you charging off to now, my boy?"

Paul was already well down the passageway outside as he called back in cheerful apology, "Sorry, Father!" His voice faded rapidly into the distance. "I'm going to the stables!"

Amused, Purwell closed the door after his rumbustious son and moved to the bed to sit by Diana. He took her hand and she smiled with pleasure.

"How are you feeling, my dear?" he enquired, then saw the handmade charm still caught up in her fingers; he touched it, inquisitively. "May I...?" Diana nodded, and sensed her father lift the pendant from her. "Where did you get it?" he asked gently.

"Todman made it," she told him, "and Mortenhurze wore it."

"Last night?"

"He rode out to find the Moon Stallion."

Purwell could see from her face that prising information from Diana wasn't going to be easy; it was more than possible that the very strangeness of the night's experience had clouded her memory of the event – mercifully, in the circumstances. No one had dared to ask yet how she had known where Mortenhurze had died, where she had found the riderless horse, or even why she had left the house to walk alone on the Downs at midnight. Whatever had happened must still hold some terror for the child, and had to be handled gently; she had to find her own way to an explanation, and Purwell was prepared to be patient. But her words reminded him of Mortenhurze's obsession with the Moon Stallion and the implied menace of its superstition; was it in some way linked to last night's tragedy?

"The beast of ill-omen…" he mused. "Was this some sort of charm for protection?"

"He didn't understand," Diana murmured. "Such a charm could never be enough."

Purwell felt compelled to be more direct; he was close to something important, if only Diana would speak openly. "Diana…" His hand held hers, seeking and offering trust. "What was it that drove Mortenhurze to his death?" He could sense her struggling to explain, but she seemed able to answer only in riddles.

"He made a challenge and lost," she answered simply.

"You aren't telling me everything," he countered.

"I… can't."

He paused and drew back from asking more questions; a change of tack was needed.

"Did Paul tell you I've found Mount Badon?" he asked cheerfully. Diana smiled and nodded.

"Yes," she said. "I was very pleased."

"It was where your dream figure pointed – to the south!" He was about to explain how he had travelled back from Liddington and, in losing his way, found the unthought-of village accidentally, when her voice cut across him.

"Then perhaps my second dream will come true as well," she murmured, and her face grew clear and thoughtful at the memory. Again Purwell knew he was close to revelation.

"You saw the Dark Rider again?"

She nodded eagerly as memory stirred, now tempered with a certain understanding.

"And great ancient empires – magnificent at first, then in ruins. Later, our own world, the twentieth century, dominated by machines…" Her father was amused and disbelieving.

"How can machines ever completely replace the horse and the skills of men?" he exclaimed, but her continuing explanation forced him to acknowledge his own uneasiness about the future of the century just begun, and he listened with growing concern.

"The machines made more machines," Diana said, her words breathless as the enormity of what she was saying became clearer. "Machines to serve man, to build, to transport him along roads, over the sea – through the air at speeds beyond sound…"

"Beyond sound!" Purwell's amazement was no longer amused. Diana's face grew more serious.

"They were huge, powerful – but deathbringers. Machines that destroyed their own world… our future world…" She paused, tragically, then went on, "Only the natural things survived – but they were changed, crippled… different. And they renewed themselves as best they could – men, women, their animals, the seeds of a new way of life…"

Purwell had caught her mood, and images of the great civilisations of the past drifted through his mind:

immense cities, glorious temples of religion and learning, supreme rulers of the known world, of Egypt, Greece, Rome – all of them corrupted and destroyed by their own vast power. A line of poetry nudged his mind, and he grimaced at its meaning, double-edged, at the sonorous warning of an inscription carved on the huge statue of an ancient, mighty king, crumbling and decayed with time: "Look on my works, ye Mighty, and despair!"

He must have said the line aloud, for Diana took him up on it.

"No, Father – despair is wrong!" Now it was her hands that gripped his in eager reassurance. "Man will always survive. The forces of the natural world about us will it to be so!"

Purwell, astonished and excited, questioned the blind child gently. "The Dark Rider told you that?"

"He was there with them," she recalled. "He rode the Moon Stallion… to lead them, to show the horse had a purpose once more, but more than that…" She paused, gathering her thoughts. "It was to show that man, beast and earth… are all part of the same existence…" Her voice trailed into silence, but Purwell's mind echoed and re-echoed with her words; who or what had put such meaning into the mouth of a child?

"The Dark Rider –" he demanded tensely, "– who is he?" The answer was immediate.

"The once and future king."

"But – that's a legend!" Purwell's mind struggled to take in the impossible idea; if what Diana was saying had any truth at all, it meant that the past, present and future were an immense wheel, with no beginning, no end, forever in motion…

"He's somewhere in these hills," Diana continued, blithely ignorant of the turmoil in her father's mind, "waiting. The stallion, too. Together, they served *her* – and when they do return, they'll lead us back to understanding."

"But who is it that they serve?" Purwell whispered.

Diana could only answer with a liturgy that conjured up the goddess without calling her by name direct. "The chalk horse is her sign… the stallion is her messenger… and Mortenhurze became the needful sacrifice."

"My father died in a riding accident!" The young voice that cut harshly across Diana's brooding words belonged to Estelle. She stood in the doorway, boldly challenging the blind girl's inner vision.

"Yes," agreed Diana, simply. Estelle knew only the reality of things; it was her whole world, and it must be respected. The truth of what Diana knew was not for her. Purwell looked from one girl to the other, unable to understand his daughter's about-face; Estelle's version of the tragedy was just as impossible!

"But what you've just said –" he began. Estelle cut him short, politely stepping aside from the open door to make her meaning quite clear.

"I wish to speak to Diana, please… alone."

"Please, Father." The sympathy in the blind girl's face was explanation enough. "It's necessary."

"Of course." Purwell squeezed Diana's hand; and,

with a kindly nod towards Estelle, left the room and quietly shut the door behind him. Estelle moved to the bed slowly. Sitting on its edge, she took Diana's hands in her own; then, with a convulsive sob, pitched forward against the blind girl's heart and wept.

*

Paul had found Todman in Rollo's stall, grooming the fine horse to gleaming perfection. At first it was clear the stable-master had no time for idle conversation, and Paul was left to stand and watch, wondering how he could possibly broach the questions in his mind. At last the currying brush was finished with; and, as Todman checked and cleared out the frog of each hoof, Paul took his chance and spoke.

"He's a beauty, isn't he?"

"The master knew the best when he saw it," Todman replied, his concentration on the task before him; but Paul sensed that, for a moment at least, the stable-master was prepared to admit the boy's presence and respond to it.

"Does the horse know, do you think?"

Todman set down one hoof, and glanced at the beast's fine build admiringly before taking up the next hoof to be handled. "They usually do," he said. "This one's lucky, mind."

"How d'you mean?" asked Paul, intrigued, as the calloused hands worked swiftly and surely on the hoof held clenched between the stable-master's knees.

"In the olden days, the steed was buried with his master."

165

"What a terrible waste!" Paul exclaimed.

"Not to their way of thinking," came the blunt reply. "The masters have need of the horse, on the other side."

Paul saw the reasoning behind this, and nodded. He'd met many such practices around the world, during his father's investigations into the ancient past.

"The Egyptians buried food and wine and slaves to look after their dead," he stated knowledgeably, but Todman wasn't impressed.

"I'm not talking about foreign parts," he said curtly. "In these very hills, I mean." He moved over to the third leg to be worked on, and Paul followed him, voicing his astonishment.

"Horses... buried with their masters?"

"Past imagining, is it?" The stable-master threw the boy a dry glance, as he cleaned the hoof smartly. "Ask your clever dad if he don't know the legend of Silbury Hill!" A pause in his work; a harder stare. "Or mebbe that blind sister o' yours knows."

Paul fell silent; suddenly he knew he dared not say too much about Diana, for fear of the stable-master's glinting anger, or perhaps worse still, his searing scorn. Deftly finishing off the final hoof, Todman glanced over his shoulder at the boy and sneered.

"Been spinning yarns again, has she?"

"No," lied Paul, defensively. "She can't seem to remember a thing." He stepped aside as Todman left the stall to move across to the tackroom, giving the boy a hard, probing look as he passed close by. Paul followed him, a few paces to the rear, and Todman flung a blunt comment back at him.

"Let's hope that's the truth of it," he grunted. Reaching the tackroom, Paul made to follow Todman inside, but with a swift turn, the stable-master had shut the lower half-door, effectively keeping the boy outside. "No admittance today, Master Purwell – I've work to do." His hard eyes dared the boy to argue.

"Can't I help?" Paul pleaded, but Todman shook his head firmly, and indicated a pile of tack waiting to be cleaned and burnished.

"Rollo's tack for the master's funeral," he explained. "Only *I* touch that."

He realised that Paul wasn't listening; the boy's gaze was pitched deeper into the shadowy tackroom, fixed on the scrying pit and the brasses scattered there. They would mean nothing to the boy, but his curiosity was obviously aroused, and Todman casually stepped into his line of sight. Paul wasn't to be put off, however. One of the brasses he had glimpsed was a crescent moon, and he was willing to swear it was identical to the one on the charm in Diana's room.

"Those old brasses – there, on the floor," he pointed out. "Aren't they supposed to be good luck charms?"

Todman's voice was soft, his eyes like steel. "Who put that into your head, boy?"

"Isn't that why they're hung onto a horse's harness?" insisted the boy, apparently innocently, "– for protection?" The stable-master glared at the boy, sizing up whether he knew the truth or not. If he did know, and was trying to be clever, then the notion must've come from the girl... and she had the talisman somewhere about her still!

The trap, freshly furbished, rolled slowly into view beyond Paul, the sound taking his attention for one brief moment. Todman slipped outside, closing both half-doors of the forbidden tackroom smartly, pretending not to see Paul's look of irritation. "Something I must see to, Master Purwell," the stable-master stated with a bland smile. "Care to walk the trap round to the front with me?" His eyes were cold as he explained drily, "Sam's driving Miss Estelle and the old biddy into Shrivenham, to make arrangements for the funeral."

Sullenly, Paul stood by as Todman checked the horse and trap with a meticulous eye for detail; Sam knew only too well the standards he had to meet and had brought both beast and vehicle up to spanking trim, so that in the event they passed Todman's close inspection with flying colours. A curt nod from the stable-master and Sam drove off, walking the horse round to the front of the house. Todman strutted along after it, a critical eye on Sam's handling, and Paul slouched along behind him, dejected at having discovered so little from the wily horse-master. His face brightened, however, as he saw his father coming down the portico steps, and the boy dashed past the elegant trap to greet his parent warmly.

"Anything planned, Father?" the boy asked eagerly. Purwell could see Paul was at a loose end and disconsolate; with Estelle wrapped up in her own personal tragedy, and Diana still recuperating from her night's mysterious adventure, there was little or nothing to occupy the youngster. But there was much that Purwell wanted to discuss, not least the question of where Todman stood in the matter of the Moon Stallion and the death of Mortenhurze. He took Paul's arm, aware that the shrewd eye of the stable-master was watching them, although he was apparently occupied with the last-minute rebuckling of a harness strap.

"I thought I'd take a stroll in the gardens," he said amiably. "Perhaps you'd like to come with me?" The grip on his arm told Paul that Purwell wanted his company on this little excursion, and the boy saw that this could be an opportunity to explain Diana's fears about Todman and the toad-bone ceremony.

"I'd like that, Father," he said, "– and there's something I'd like to show you…"

They marched off together; and, straightening up, Todman watched them into the distance with narrowed eyes. A plan was forming in his mind, which, with father and son out of the way and a touch of luck, could turn disaster into triumph.

A nod told Sam to wait, and Todman stepped briskly into the cool shadows of the hallway. Mrs Brookes was there, veiled and in black, ready to go out; she nodded stiffly to the stable-master as he took off his cap and saluted her politely.

"Sam's ready to take you and Miss Estelle, ma'am," he said. His eyes flickered up the sweep of the wrought-iron staircase, with its polished banister of rich, dark wood, and the housekeeper responded to the unspoken question.

"Thank you, Mr Todman, she'll not be a minute."

Todman fussed with his cap, and gave an approving nod. "Taken it like a little lady, hasn't she?"

"She's her father's daughter – a proper Mortenhurze," declared Mrs Brookes warmly. "Strong and proud and plenty of grit, that's what they've got!"

Todman fidgeted, playing even more nervously with his cap, giving the impression he was out of place and would sooner be on his way. His eyes asked Mrs Brookes to be understanding, and she obliged, affably.

"If you don't mind me not waiting, ma'am…?"

"I know you've got work to do, Mr Todman," she replied solemnly. "Carry on, if you will."

With a jerk of his head, Todman indicated the passageway that led past the stairs and into the working quarters of the huge house, and gave a quizzical smile. "All right if I go through the kitchens, is it?"

Mrs Brookes, distracted by Estelle coming down the great stairs, gave a brusque nod of permission, and the stable-master slipped quickly away, out of sight among the shadows of the inner passage. A minute later, Estelle and the housekeeper had gone and the huge hall door had closed. Not until the sound of the trap's wheels on the gravel drive had faded into silence did Todman step out from hiding; then, with a look of grim purpose, he made his way swiftly up the stairs that would lead him to the blind girl's room.

Chapter Thirteen

FROM THE UPPER WINDOWS OF the house, the formal gardens could be seen spread out below like a boldly patterned carpet laid out in the early summer sun. It was past noon now, and a drowsy stillness shimmered in the warm air. The distant figure of a gardener hunched over the weedless perfection of a bed of tulips; a wandering cock pheasant strutted lazily across the farthest lawn, before clattering into flight from the only two other figures passing innocently through his kingdom, deep in conversation.

Todman looked out furtively, careful not to be seen, his flinty eyes narrowed against the soft glare of the sunshine. He gave a thin smile as he recognised Purwell and his son walking towards the cascading rhododendrons that filled the far shrubbery with royal colour; the pieces were falling into place, luck was on his side, but now he must act quickly.

He turned from the window, and lithe and silent as a cat moved along the landing corridor until he came to the door he wanted; a pause, and then, like a shadow, he opened the door and slipped inside the room.

"Who is it?" questioned Diana, her blind face bright with expectation, hoping for another morning visitor. There was no answer, and she frowned. She knew the door had opened, sensed that someone was in the room, that she was no longer alone. But why was there no answer to her question? "Please tell me."

Todman ignored her. Aware that the blind child had no way of knowing who he was, he moved boldly and openly about the bedroom, eyes searching keenly for that which didn't belong here, which was his by right: the moon charm. At last he saw it, resting on the bedside table next to the sprig of mistletoe, and with a sudden, greedy movement, snatched it up. Diana, alert but not afraid, heard the swift rustle of movement and knew what it meant.

"Mister Todman!" Her face was turned towards the side of the bed where he was standing, and he froze, wondering how those blind eyes could know so much. "You've come to take back the moon charm," she said.

He straightened and his chin lifted arrogantly. She had no power over him, strange though she might be; he had the talisman now, while she was blind, helpless and alone in an almost deserted house. Even if she were to scream aloud, the sound would go unnoticed, quickly muffled by the doors and walls between her and the occasional servant scurrying about her work below stairs. Todman smiled; he was the master here.

"How did you come by it?" he demanded, glancing at the talisman to see if it had been tampered with; it had not, but he was still uneasy. Her reply was no comfort.

"I was there when Mortenhurze found what he was seeking," Diana said calmly. "The charm couldn't save him."

Todman's mind grew cold. *She had been there when Mortenhurze had found the Moon Stallion.* Yet he was dead and she was not – why? What had she to gain? If she was not a rival to be feared, nor a secret whisperer who had stumbled across his star-path in error… His confusion turned to anger, and he rasped at her, furiously questioning.

"What *are* you? What charm protects you?" He snatched up the sprig of golden, drying mistletoe. "This? It means nothing!" He glared at the blind girl, his breath tight in his throat. She did not fear him.

"It's the Golden Bough," she said, Todman's mind seethed with questions at the naming of that ancient symbol.

"Who gave it to you, girl?" he demanded.

"The Green King," came the calm reply.

The horse-master stared at the blind girl with awe and anger in his eyes. She had met the Old One face to face – and lived. Small but powerful, this golden wand had been her only protection: now it was his! Quickly he slipped the sprig of mistletoe inside his shirt, as she appealed to him.

"I'm not your rival," she insisted quietly. "I have no power. But you must turn back!"

"You know my purpose, do you?" sneered the horsemaster. He placed the bone and silver talisman about his neck, and all his pride returned as the blind girl revealed how little she really knew.

"You want to charm the Moon Stallion!"

Todman laughed quietly, then paused, studying Diana's puzzled face before boasting, "Girl, I seek more power than that!"

She gave a tiny gasp of dismay as she saw the wildness of his dark ambition – it was madness.

"The Moon Goddess?" she whispered, "You dare not command *her*!"

Todman saw something like panic in the blind girl's face, and asked shrewdly. "What is she to you?"

"I share her name," Diana replied simply. "She rules my birth sign."

Todman responded to her words by echoing the Green King's lunar incantation. "The stallion is only a symbol of her power," he declared. "She rules the tides of Fate, the Wheel of Being –" his voice dropped to a vibrant, vehement whisper, "– but when I ride the Moon Stallion, the goddess will obey *me*!"

He looked into the Moon Child's face , and his heart leapt with joy as he saw another fragment of the mystery fall into place. The girl wasn't a threat: she had been sent to him *to be used*! Suddenly purposeful, he pulled out a large kerchief from his pocket, and kneeling on the bedcover, started to gag her. Her protests were quickly stifled, and she made only a token struggle as Todman's strong fingers did their work.

"It is you who will bring the Moon Stallion to me!" he whispered, his lean mouth cruel against her ear. She turned her head towards him in alarm, but he had already moved away. A quick search of the room revealed her travelling cloak hanging on the back of the door. Half-lifting, half-dragging her from the bed, he flung the cloak around her clumsily.

"Beltane isn't ended yet," he said darkly; then, as she stumbled, he lifted her fragile weight and carried her without effort in muscular arms. He looked into her unseeing eyes and smiled, cold and sardonic.

"If you *are* the Moon Child," he said, "the stallion will come!"

*

The first stage of Todman's escape was to the stables, and it was quickly and easily accomplished. Even with the burden of the girl, he moved swiftly, making his way down the stairs and along the passageways of the rear of the house like a shadow. A passing scullery maid sent Todman huddling into an open cupboard doorway, but the danger was soon past and within minutes he had loped across the stable yard and brought Diana into Rollo's stall, where no one but the stable-master himself was normally allowed.

Setting the helpless girl to one side, Todman deftly saddled the waiting horse; it blew quietly, aware that a ride was in the offing, eager to be free of the dim stall. Todman watched a lad walk a horse across the otherwise deserted yard towards the paddock, and, in the silence that followed, brought Rollo out, with Diana already in the saddle, clinging tightly. Stirrup turned to take his foot, a swift easy rise and the horse-master was in the saddle behind her, steadying her and urging the chestnut stallion into a canter before opening into a full gallop as they reached the grassy parkland. Within minutes they were out of sight, riding hard across the Downs and towards the distant White Horse Hill, safe in the knowledge that no one had seen Todman or his captive go.

They paused only once, as Todman gave the horse a breather and at the same time took the gag from the blind girl's mouth.

"Shout if you must," he grunted sardonically. "There's no one'll hear you now."

"Where are we?" asked Diana.

"Two miles from Dragon Hill," he answered curtly, and rode on. Before long they reached Alfred's Hill, and, riding beside the hedgerows, made their way between the outskirts of Uffington village to the north and Woolstone to the south and west. A hard turn to the right brought them quickly to the winding lane that rose between Dragon Hill and the great chalk image looming over it. Todman glanced up at it to his left; sensing his movement, Diana twisted towards him as he reined the horse in for a brief moment.

"Are we there?" she asked.

"Epona's sign is over us," he replied. "We'll be there soon."

It was impossible to take in all the mighty image of the horse at this close range and the horse-master waited no longer. Within seconds he had ridden the horse to the track that would lead them to the crest of the earthwork fortress; when at last they reached the uppermost point, Todman halted the horse, lowered the blind girl to the ground and then himself dismounted. He dropped the horse's reins over its head, letting it walk away to graze, no longer needed.

The horse-master stood, stern and arrogant, gazing all about him from the magnificent vantage point high on the flank of White Horse Hill. At his feet knelt Diana; his hand on her shoulder kept her in her place. Half-turning her head, she questioned him.

"Why are you so sure the Moon Stallion will come?"

"Because I know its nature," came the dour assertion, "and because I will it so."

Diana felt a whisper of fear – not for herself but for the man behind her, so desperate for secret power that he was blind to danger. She knew also that warning him was useless; he had no faith in strangers, only in himself.

"If you go on, you are lost," she said calmly.

"You're a child. You know nothing," he retorted.

"I know you need the toad bone. And it is all you have."

Todman glared down at her, then crouched by her side, his face so close to hers that she flinched. With the cord still about his neck, he brought the bone and silver talisman out from his shirt and touched it against her cheek. She gasped and turned away as though from something icy-cold. He chuckled, cruelly.

"You feel its mystery, do you?"

"In your hands, it's an evil thing!"

He drew back slightly, letting the talisman fall onto his chest. Kneeling, he still dominated the child.

"Then you know what I am," he said.

Diana nodded. "A horse warlock."

"A master of horses!" boasted Todman. "*All* horses!"

"The Moon Stallion, too?"

"That one most of all…" The dark-eyed warlock brooded, his mind thinking only of that moment when he alone would ride the wild white horse.

"You think you can force it to obey you?" Diana interrupted his thoughts with her question, and Todman frowned.

"*When* it obeys me –" he told her in a fierce whisper, "– all the secrets of nature will be open to me. I will rule the wind and water, earth and fire. I will speak with the beasts and make the very minds of living things serve only me!" He paused, letting his arrogant gaze take in the world that would soon be his, and his eyes flashed proudly. "I will be the greatest warlock of all time!"

"No one can rule the Moon Goddess!"

"But there is a way to share her power," retorted Todman. "By rite of combat!"

Diana tensed with alarm at the horse-master's supreme confidence and his knowledge of so many hidden things. The Green King had been right – Todman was a danger that had to be faced and conquered, for his ways were evil.

"You dare to challenge the Green King, Wayland –
her champion?" demanded the blind girl.

"He is a dying tree," said Todman, "and he will fall."

"But his power is renewed!" Diana cried. "He will
destroy you!"

The warlock dismissed her warning with a contemp-
tuous shake of his head. "He will try – for that is the law
of the sacred grove. But if he fails… *I take his place!*"

Now Diana recalled with dismay the legend of the
sacred grove: how in ancient times the circlet of trees
dedicated to Diana, Goddess of the Hunt and of the
Moon, was guarded by a man chosen as her hermit priest
and earthly husband – the choosing bound to a cruel
yearly ritual. Once a year a challenger would come,
demanding to serve the goddess himself; only the strong
survived, for this was a fight to the death, and the
challenger could not be refused. The ritual had long
since died with the passing of those ancient gods, but
now Todman had rediscovered it, here in these time-
locked hills, and with his secret powers had brought the
Green King back from his long sleep for one evil
purpose: to usurp the priest-magician's power. Diana
shivered with fear. In Todman's hands, what would that
power become?

"Once I am the Green King," he crooned, "I will be
priest to her goddess, her consort, master of her magic –
all-powerful!" He laughed. "And the Moon Stallion is all
I need to make the final challenge!" He stood, and,
cupping his hands to his mouth, called into the wind,
wild-eyed and insolent. "Moon Stallion! I am your

master! Come… to… me!"

On all the hills around, there was no sound, no sign of movement, not one answering echo to the warlock's call. The lean cast of his face became even more bitter, as Diana voiced his secret fear.

"It won't come to you now… not in daylight."

"It showed itself to *you* before." He glared at her venomously. "And the power of Beltane lasts till midnight!"

"Mortenhurze is dead," Diana stated flatly. "You have failed."

"A sacrifice had to be made," retorted Todman. "It was Mortenhurze who failed!"

"You sent him… in your place?" wondered the blind girl, beginning to realise what the horse-master had done, and that he would stick at nothing.

"To open the way." The remark was off-hand, ruthless.

"But he was an *unwilling* sacrifice!"

Todman didn't need to be reminded; it was a risk he'd had to take. The blind girl knew too much, she was making him angry. "The offering was made – let that be enough!"

Diana would not be shouted down; the ancient law was clear. Todman was a condemned man.

"By betraying him, you defiled the Beltane rite!" she cried, defying him for all her weakness.

Furiously, he pointed a lean, stabbing finger down at Dragon Hill far below, and almost screamed at the Moon Child, "He died on *her* altar, in *her* name!"

"But he was an intruder," Diana calmly insisted, her blind face turned towards him, Justice with uncovered eyes. He could not bear that blank, eerily soul-searching stare, and turned away with a defensive mutter.

"The ancient law allows –"

She cut him short, quietly relentless. "No – he was driven here, hounded to destruction by her own avengers... the Wild Hunt." Todman was drawn back to her by her accusation, full of sad truth. "And at the last, Mortenhurze knew why..."

"The price is paid!" He stared at her with growing fear, then broke away, desperately scanning the empty hills. "What I ask in return *must be given!*"

An ancient voice sounded deep in Diana's mind, forming the words of mystery on her young lips. As the words came, Todman turned and, looking down at her, saw her straighten and tremble slightly, aware of a secret coming... She smiled.

"The stallion is her messenger... the sign he brings will be your answer."

"You know something –" Todman rasped. He took her wrist violently. "Tell me!"

Calmly, drawn by Todman's cruel strength, Diana rose to her feet. Without hesitation, she turned and pointed blindly to the crest of the hill behind them. Standing there, where seconds before there was nothing, was the Moon Stallion, proud and unmoving. Todman saw, and his senses sang with triumph.

"At last!" he whispered, pushing Diana from him. She fell to her knees and crouched there, listening intently, aware of something unknown and terrible, but holding no fear for her. Todman stepped forward slowly, confronting the magic horse, the talisman held in his hand but its thong still around his neck. Crooning softly, he commanded the stallion to him, but it made no move.

"Your master bids you, Moon Stallion!" His voice grew harder, without mercy. "Come to me – *now!*" He straightened, eyes bright with excitement, as slowly the stallion walked forward… closer… then *past* the enraged horse-master to the kneeling girl behind him. Todman whirled to confront Diana, his extended hand trembling with fury.

"Bring the horse *to me!*"

"He has given his message," she replied. "Go back, while you can."

Todman ignored the warning. Step by step, he moved towards the girl and the stallion standing at her side; his rage only increased as she rose to her feet and blindly fondled the sleek head nuzzling her shoulder.

"Obey me!"

Neither the stallion nor Diana moved. Todman took a step closer, toad bone held out before him, his eyes wary of the stallion's mood.

"I have the right!" demanded the warlock in a voice choked with desperation. Suddenly, he swallowed hard as the blind girl spoke, one hand gently resting on the stallion's neck.

"It will be yours," she said, simply. Todman stood like a statue, scarcely daring to believe his ears. "But first you must know its purpose."

Todman's face grew sly, and he sidled closer slowly. "While you preach," he said, "let me mount the horse."

"No one will prevent you." As Diana spoke, Todman reached the Moon Stallion's side, and holding his breath, gently stroked its neck and shoulder. It made not a move, and the warlock's face was filled with awe and exultation. He hardly heard what the blind girl said; it was as if she wasn't there.

"The Moon Stallion is her messenger, but more than that –" Diana's voice was strangely calm, clear as crystal, "– it is the Death Horse."

Todman was already on the stallion's back; he looked down at the blind girl and she meant nothing to him.

"It cannot harm me – I am its master now!"

"It will take you where it must –" uttered Diana, giving voice to the shadows in her mind, "– not where you choose."

Scornfully, Todman waved aside her ominous words. "It obeys me!" he cried, revelling in his new-found power. "See how it moves to my touch!" He moved the horse this way and that with knee and heel, hand on mane, while Diana stood stock-still at the centre of the stallion's quiet perambulations.

"It will take me to the Green King," he said, "and I am not afraid!"

"Wayland's Smithy is only a gateway…"

Todman picked up Diana's solemn warning and laughed in her face. "… to Tír na nÓg, the ancient Isle of the Dead! Do you think I don't know that? The prize is worth the danger – I risk all to win all!"

"There can be no return," insisted the blind girl, but his certainty of purpose brushed her childish prediction aside almost mockingly.

"Only one of us will fail, Moon Child," Todman said. "To the loser, an eternity of darkness, but to the new champion, eternal power! The Green King must meet my challenge, now!" He wheeled the horse about, boldly displaying his new talisman, the golden bough of mistletoe. He shouted back at Diana, "But I shall be the victor!"

From nowhere, the rushing of a mighty wind tore frenziedly at the warlock's hair and clothing, sending the stallion rearing high. Nearby, Rollo threw up his head, eyes rolling, and, spooked by the eerie storm-wind, bolted wildly down the far hillside and out of sight. Todman, taking the rearing of the stallion as a challenge, delighted in using all his skills to keep his grip on the plunging animal – but suddenly, it broke into an explosive gallop that took it, mane and tail streaming in the wind, down the hillside and towards the chalk track gleaming in the distance.

Todman let the beast have its head, relishing with keen pleasure its exhilarating speed and power. His own movements became one with the rhythmic surge of the muscle and sinew thrusting beneath him, and he laughed into the wind, wild with exultation.

Then, as he made to turn the stallion in a wide arc that would take horse and rider in a racing curve around the lower ramparts of the grassy moat, he found the horse was fighting him, ignoring even the sharpest heeling of its flanks, striding inexorably onward to the course of its own choosing – onto the Ridgeway and the west, to Wayland's Smithy.

Chapter Fourteen

ONLY A FEW SHREDS OF the dead toad's skin remained, but they were evidence enough as Paul told his father about the strange ritual the children had seen Todman perform to make the toad-bone charm. Purwell had heard of the warlock superstition; it was thought to be long dead, but he had to admit that while there were horses, men would seek to master them, just as with any other needed skill.

As the boy described the details of Todman's secret ceremony and Diana's unease at what it might mean, the professor recalled the vision Diana had experienced – the rise and death of machines and the aftermath, the return of the Dark Rider. At the back of his mind Purwell sensed there was, strangely, a shared link, a bridge between the mystery of the blind girl's dream and the grim reality of Mortenhurze's death. But then the half-formed intuition slipped away, as Paul's insistent voice continued to explain.

"Diana thinks the charm wasn't just for ordinary horses –"

His father caught the meaning and wondered aloud, as he stood from crouching over the smooth stone and looked around the clearing for any other signs of ritual. "The Moon Stallion?"

"I think she's right," declared Paul. "That crescent on the charm she brought back – Todman has more. And he wasn't pleased when I saw them!"

Purwell was wary about jumping to conclusions on evidence he hadn't seen for himself. "If you mean horse brasses, Paul," he responded, "you must remember that horsemen are often very superstitious."

Paul took his chance, excitedly. "Todman says there are horses and their riders buried in these hills!"

Purwell knew instantly that the horse-master could have meant only one place, one legend. "Silbury Hill!" he exclaimed.

Paul nodded, keenly. "He told me to ask you about it; what does it mean?"

The professor recalled what he had seen of the huge earth-formed cone – called a hill, but man-made even so.

"Silbury Hill…" he mused, "… made by men, centuries ago, perhaps as far back as Wayland's Smithy or the great stone circles of Avebury…"

"Todman said there was a legend –"

Purwell's eyes grew thoughtful, clouded, as the information sprang to mind.

"A golden rider on a golden horse… inside that great mound… waiting."

Paul looked at his father in surprise, and for a moment Purwell held his glance. "But… that's part of the legend of King Arthur!"

"One of many such fragments," his father replied drily, then looked keenly at the boy as he echoed the professor's own earlier thought.

"Then if Diana is right… they're all connected!"

"A jigsaw of dark forces," brooded Purwell. "But what is Todman's part in it?"

He took Paul's arm, and slowly they began to walk back through the cool shadows of the yew hedges towards the house. Both were deep in thought, but Paul offered a suggestion, and his father nodded in agreement. "I think Diana knows, Father. Let's ask her."

Purwell glanced at the boy by his side. "Has she told you she believes that the death of Mortenhurze had something to do with the Moon Stallion?" he asked.

"Yes – and with Beltane, too?" Paul added, frowning. It seemed impossible to him that a long-forgotten Celtic feast day could still have meaning. "Father – what she said about Dragon Hill – surely it can't be true?"

"An altar to the cult of the White Horse and Epona," murmured the professor, "… with Mortenhurze as sacrifice."

"But rituals like that ended over a thousand years ago!" Paul protested. Purwell was less dogmatic.

"Traces of the Old Religion still remain, my boy," he remarked drily. "You'll find them throughout Britain –

though more usually as harmless folk customs, I'll admit."

"Could they still have power and meaning even now?" wondered the youngster.

His father didn't answer directly, but allowed the thoughts to spill freely from his mind. "Sun and Moon, life and death, Earth and its seasons... they were vital forces to ancient man."

Paul became irritated; archaeology and legends were all very well, but this was 1906! "Father –" he said pointedly, "– the Celts no longer exist!"

Purwell stopped short in his steady pacing and turned to face his son; his eyes were dark with speculation, and for a moment Paul saw the likeness to Diana.

"But suppose the power of what they once believed... *remains*?" the professor suggested soberly.

"In these hills?"

Purwell nodded and walked on, letting Diana's thinking guide his mind.

"Arthur, the immortal king, waiting for new life... the sleeping hero inside Silbury Hill... golden, untarnished... a symbol of what will be alive once more, after all destruction..."

"But how can you link Silbury with the White Horse?" demanded the puzzled boy. "It's miles away!"

The professor gave Paul a quick, excited smile, then, taking him firmly by the arm, pulled him along at a faster, more purposeful pace. "It may be closer than we think," he said. "Come along, I want to show you something!"

*

In the library Purwell held up a framed print from Mortenhurze's collection for Paul to study. The copperplate calligraphy gave the date of the drawing as 1838. Strangely, it wasn't of a horse but of a simple conical mound, yet Paul recognised it instantly and answered his father's question.

"Dragon Hill," came his confident reply.

"Wrong!" contradicted the professor, then chuckled with obvious delight. "But an excellent response!"

Paul couldn't understand what sort of game his father was playing at all. "Why are you pleased that I'm wrong?"

"Because," said Purwell mischievously, "you are looking at a print of *Silbury* Hill!" Paul looked again, and wondered, and began to see why his father was so excited.

"They're virtually identical," he admitted.

Purwell bustled to explain, using the print as his blackboard, briskly indicating form and dimensions on the tinted engraving. "Silbury is far larger, of course – some one hundred and thirty feet high – and we know it is man-made." He set the print aside, but Paul continued staring at it, mentally comparing, as his father went on: "Dragon Hill, on the other hand, has always been *assumed* to be a natural formation." He paused to give emphasis to his next remark. "But did you know that Arthur was also known in parts of Britain as – the Dragon King?"

"Dragon Hill…" wondered Paul, seeing now where

his father's thoughts were leading him. "You mean... the legend of the golden horse and rider, waiting... belongs *there*?"

Purwell nodded excitedly. "The once and future king –" he blurted out, "– buried under Dragon Hill!"

"But... what about the legend of St George?" puzzled Paul.

"A convenient Christian gentleman whose heroism in killing an unpleasant dragon was used to disguise the *true* purpose of the mound – to provide an altar for blood sacrifices to Epona at the feast of Beltane!"

Caught up in his father's bright enthusiasm, Paul couldn't help adding, "Arthur the warrior. Sleeping beneath *her* altar – his tomb marked by her sacred beast... the White Horse!"

They looked at each other, elated at the image they had conjured up, but Purwell found the thought of Mortenhurze returning to his mind, tragically. Was it coincidence that his search for the Moon Stallion had ended on Dragon Hill, Epona's altar? Or was Purwell building a false theory on what was, after all, a simple riding accident? It was Paul who broke the mood, no longer questioning but a cheerful convert to his father's earlier suggestion.

"Perhaps there *is* power in ancient places, after all."

Purwell said nothing, but let his thoughts run on as he and Paul, with one accord, headed for the library door. They entered the cool hallway and started up the stairs. It had been Diana who had sensed that power in the hills that shadowed them from the moment they first arrived, and Purwell suddenly realised he needed his daughter's intuition more than ever now; without it, he was blind.

*

Finding Diana's bedroom empty, their first reaction was surprise rather than alarm.

"Where is she?" wondered Purwell. Before his mind could recall her midnight absence and grow concerned, Paul made a reassuring discovery.

"She's taken her cloak, Father," he pointed out. Purwell smiled, understanding and relieved.

"Of course!" he exclaimed gently. "She must've gone out with Estelle and Mrs Brookes."

"She might've told us," grumbled Paul good-naturedly.

"She was more concerned about Estelle, I suspect," suggested the professor. "I left them here together – Estelle needed companionship and a chance to weep, perhaps."

"Have they gone far?" Paul asked, silently wondering if their absence meant that lunch would be delayed for long; he was feeling hungry.

"To Shrivenham – some necessary business about the funeral." Purwell smiled, guessing at the reason for Paul's concern. Don't worry, my boy – they'll be back well in time for lunch!"

Grinning, Paul drifted towards the window and looked out. "It'd be like her to put Estelle first, wouldn't it? They've been almost like sisters.

Purwell's face was serious as he nodded in agreement.

"A blessing in the circumstances."

The sound of hooves and wheels on gravel came up to them faintly, and Paul turned excitedly from the window. "They're back!" he exclaimed. "The trap's just pulling up at the front door!" He started to go towards the door with his father, then hesitated. "Are we going to tell Estelle...?" He left the rest unsaid, but Purwell understood and shook his head.

"Not yet," he said, and led the way downstairs.

*

Estelle was still in the process of unpinning her hat when Purwell and his son came down into the hallway. Her pale, drawn face looked up at him as she handed her things to Mrs Brookes; like the black-frocked housekeeper, she was wondering why Purwell's pleasant smile of greeting had faded into vague anxiety. At his father's shoulder, Paul was more direct.

"Where's Diana?" he demanded bluntly.

"She didn't come out with us," answered Estelle, mildly resenting his curt manner. "She needed to rest."

"Then where *is* she?" Purwell appealed to his son who, seeing Estelle's frown, hastened to explain.

"Diana isn't in her room," he stated.

Mrs Brookes lifted the mourning veil from her wide-brimmed hat to reveal a look of stern surprise. "She's never sleepwalking again?"

"In daylight?" Estelle reproved the housekeeper with a cool glance, then turned to the professor, gently sympathetic. He was flustered, trying to conceal his agitation.

"Her travelling cloak is missing," he said.

"Perhaps she's sitting in the gardens?" Estelle suggested. Paul cut in restlessly.

"We've been there nearly all the time!"

"It's broad daylight," countered Estelle. "*Someone* must've seen her."

"Mister Todman –" suggested the housekeeper, "perhaps he knows, miss." She went on to explain. "He was in the house – just before we left for Shrivenham –"

"Todman!" exclaimed Paul, turning to his father with desperate eyes. Purwell's face darkened.

"If *he* has had a hand in this –"

"I'm going to find out!" cried Paul, and dashed out into the afternoon sunshine.

*

In the stable yard Sam had barely started getting down to unharnessing the horse from the trap when Paul burst upon him, full of questions, followed by the professor and Estelle. Bemused, Sam had to ask another stable lad before he could be sure of his answer.

"Mister Todman isn't here," came his slow reply. Paul turned to the others as they reached him, their faces anxious to know what, if anything, he'd discovered.

"Todman's gone too!" shouted Paul.

Something made Estelle turn towards Rollo's stall across the yard; and, noticing that both half-doors were fully open, she ran to it, picking up her skirts. It was empty. She spun about to confront Purwell and his son as they hurried after her, and her eyes blazed.

"He's taken Rollo!" she cried angrily. "Father's

horse!"

But Purwell was looking beyond her. Easing his way past her slight figure, he entered the stall and, crouching, picked up a small piece of fine linen, lace-edged, and held it up for the others to see. It was Diana's handkerchief.

"He has her with him!" muttered Purwell, his face tragic. Estelle stared at him in dismay.

"But where would he take her?"

"Wayland's Smithy!" Paul blurted out, confidently. "Where she last saw the Moon Stallion!"

Estelle's wan face shadowed with surprise. "He wants it… still?" she asked. Purwell got to his feet and tucked the tiny handkerchief into his jacket pocket as he turned to Estelle soberly.

"There are dark forces at work here, Estelle," he said quietly. "We must find Diana before it's too late."

"We must have horses – quickly!" Paul started towards the nearby stalls, but checked at Estelle's tense voice.

"Father was found at Dragon Hill," she reminded them bravely. "Someone should go there, too."

For one grim second Paul and his father stood motionless, numbed by the meaning behind Estelle's remark; then, aware that there was no time to lose, they sprang into action. While Paul and Estelle organised horses for themselves, Purwell stormed across the stable yard towards Sam, who watched their frenzied activity with mouth agape and puzzled eyes. Unceremoniously Purwell bundled him into reharnessing the trap, as he called to the youngsters across the yard.

"I'll take the trap to White Horse Hill!" Then he turned on Sam, commanding tersely, "Hurry up, boy! You're coming with me!"

Chapter Fifteen

THE GREAT WIND NO LONGER raged across the bleak
ramparts of the earthwork fortress, but neither had it
died completely. Diana could still sense its quiet power
all about her, contained yet ready to pounce like a huge
invisible cat upon its fragile prey, murmuring and
moaning in soft expectation. Beyond the low keening of
that eerie wind, there was nothing; both Rollo and the
Moon Stallion were lost to all her senses and she knew
that she was utterly alone. She stood quite still, turning a
brave face to the sulking wind, but its changing direction
constantly eluded her. It had struck before, but it had left
her untouched at Wayland's Smithy. There she had been
protected; here she was not.

She shivered, and slipped to her knees, huddling
deeper into her cloak, unable to escape the chilling cold
of something even more menacing than the wind. The

force that Todman had unwittingly released was cruel and savage, yet also cunning as the darkest side of nature's mind; she was its prisoner, an intruder to be lightly held and dealt with later, once Todman the warlock had been set aside.

For the second time on White Horse Hill, she was afraid. In full daylight there was no protection for a Moon Child here; her golden talisman – the sprig of mistletoe – was lost to her, and without it she could expect no help from the Green King either. He was rooted to his kingdom of the dead, just as were the ancient trees guarding the sacred grove, and he ruled only within the boundary of their branches. The Moon Stallion, too, had its own task and couldn't be recalled; it was the Death Horse bearing Todman to his destiny, and until that was done it could have no other purpose. Diana's only hope seemed puny in comparison – Paul and her father, brave but pitifully human to be pitted against the threat of the unknown. She smiled wryly to herself; they probably didn't even know that she'd been kidnapped. Before long the wind that was the Wild Hunt would return to White Horse Hill and claim her for its own. Until then, she could only wait – and hope.

*

The trap had been the first to be properly harnessed up and ready to go; it drove off furiously without waiting for Estelle or Paul, rattling out of the stable yard, along the driveway sweeping through the drowsing parkland and into the twisting lanes beyond. Encouraged by the professor's eagerness, Sam drove with an urgency that pushed horse and vehicle to their utmost limits, taking corners with an abandon that had Purwell holding on for dear life. The youngsters were soon mounted and followed hard along the lanes behind the trap, before breaking off across open countryside to take their separate route to the west of Crompton Beauchamp and the steep rise of Odstone Hill. For a moment, before they parted company with Purwell at a point just beyond Longcot, he could see them riding the hill above the road, and he waved to them, bravely. An instant later they had galloped out of sight over the hill's skyline, and with a yelp of alarm the professor grabbed at Sam's shoulder, reminding him to keep his excited eyes on the road ahead and not on the departing riders to his right. The nearside wheel of the speeding trap had bitten well into the roadside verge before Sam had brought it back to a safer course in answer to Purwell's anxious cry.

"Look where you're going, boy!" he shouted, but without hesitation encouraged the eager stable-lad to even greater efforts. "And faster – faster!"

Sam, wild-eyed and grinning broadly, needed little or no urging; his blood was up, and whatever it was that they were chasing, he'd do his damnedest to make sure he and the professor were first in at the kill! With a great whoop, Sam leaned forward and cracked his whip, driving like a racing charioteer as the trap entered the long straight that led into and through Woolstone village – and there, little more than a mile ahead, was the looming hulk of White Horse Hill.

*

Trapped in the shadowed green tunnel of the Ridgeway, Todman fought desperately to turn the stallion's head and change the furiously galloping beast's direction, but it was useless. The wind searing at his face and trailing in the horse's wake seemed to carry in its raging breath more than the sound of the stallion's own hooves, pounding along the chalky highway; there were a hundred other horsemen riding at his heels – but when Todman turned his head to look, the Ridgeway was menacing and empty. Whatever pursued him was invisible, and a sudden fear gripped him as he caught sight of the hedgerow rushing past – *not a leaf moved, all was still, untouched by that eerie wind*! Close to panic now, he tried again to wrench the stallion's head about, but it strode relentlessly onward, never shifting from its appointed course.

Like a nightmare echo, the blind girl's voice came back to him: "It will take you where it must –" she had said, "– not where you choose!" His breath tightened in his throat, and he clutched the stallion's mane more tightly. If the Wild Hunt had driven Mortenhurze onto the altar of Dragon Hill, where would it take Todman now? With a lurching heart he sensed that the stallion was at last about to change its path; and, in a turn so tight that it defied belief, the horse abruptly plunged into the gap that led to Wayland's Smithy. In three strides it had jumped the gate there, and pulled up to a breathless halt in the centre of the sacred grove.

Inside the glade of tall mysterious trees there was no wind at all. Outside, the day was soft with May sunshine and the haze of distant hills, but beneath those branches darkness seemed to gather like a coming thunderstorm. The stallion, proudly facing the sarsen stones guarding the entrance to the tomb, lowered its sleek head as though in greeting, and Todman looked all about him, dark-eyed and alert. There was no one there; the place was deserted, wrapped in a silence so cold that it crushed the soul. Suddenly, out of the imprisoning tangle of branches high overhead, a sullen rumble of thunder drifted downwards into the eerie glade; and, hearing it, the caged warlock stared upward in alarm. Not a bird was there, not a single shaft of sunlight filtered through, and his mind clenched tight with fear. His gaze slid down to the tomb once more.

He was not alone.

Facing him in brutal majesty was the bold silhouette of the Green King, a burly shadow set against the aura of the Beltane fire that pulsed and glowed behind him. Todman desperately fought back his rising fear; his eyes saw with chilling disbelief the great horned helmet that, in the flickering bale-fire, could have been antlers or even the twisted branches of an ancient tree. A smith's hammer, gripped tightly in one gnarled and gauntleted fist, told Todman who this grim adversary was – and the voice that challenged him was as harsh and as resonant as beaten iron.

"The horse you ride is mine!" it rang out. Todman sat on the stallion bravely, his lean body defiant and erect, all fear hidden by bold arrogance.

"You stand in my way, Green King!" he cried, staking

everything on the final gamble.

"This is my ground," echoed the stern reply, "the gateway to darkness. Do you dare to ride on?"

"Todman the warlock defies you!" The horse-master watched almost without breathing as the mighty hammer was lifted to point directly at his chest.

"With charms and trinkets?"

Todman did not flinch, but met the glowering authority of Wayland with flinty eyes.

"You know my purpose here, Old One," he rasped. "Accept my challenge!"

"I deny you your right!" the Green King growled in answer, scornfully. "Epona has set her face against you!"

"The ancient law cannot be denied!"

"You have betrayed that law," retorted Wayland. "Your sacrifice is tainted; your mind is evil; your hands are unclean! You are doomed!"

"You are at the sunset of your years, Old One," snarled the warlock. "Act as you know you must, or crawl back into that kingdom of worms and darkness that is your tomb! Fight for your sacred crown – now!"

The Green King looked on the warlock with infinite weariness, and raised the hammer of Thor again. "No man may challenge me and live," he said; but before the sacred thunderbolt could strike, Todman's harsh command rang out across the clearing, boldly. His arm thrust outward, and in his fingers was the dull gold of the shaft of mistletoe; Todman's eyes glared past that innocent talisman, and their gaze was venom.

"By this sacred talisman," he cried, "I bind your

power!" The hammer trembled in Wayland's mighty fist, but it would rise no further. Seeing what Todman held, the priest-king started.

"The Golden Bough!" His surprise changed to deep concern as he realised how Todman must have come by it, and the danger that must now surround Diana. "Without it, the Moon Child is defenceless!"

"That is no concern of mine," retorted Todman. "She has served her purpose!"

"You betray all that you touch, warlock," growled Wayland wearily. "She was the link between us."

"She was there to be used!"

"But not to be sacrificed!"

Todman was growing bitter and impatient. "She is nothing. I am here and the challenge has been made. Answer!"

"I accept," the Green King nodded, curtly. "That is the law."

"Put down the symbols of your power," commanded Todman.

Slowly, his piercing eyes never leaving the warlock's face, Wayland discarded first the shield of knowledge in whose burnished depths Diana had seen so many mysteries, then the richly worked and golden-horned helmet of justice. Todman, his eyes now filled with greed, watched as that potent sceptre of the priest-king's authority was gently laid on the ground between them, and let his thoughts be known.

"Who holds the hammer next will be its master," he gloated. Wayland was unimpressed.

"No talismans, no words of power, no magic – that is the law. The combat between us must be by human force alone, hand to hand, as it was in ancient time."

Arrogantly, Todman tossed the sprig of mistletoe onto the ground, but still the Green King was not satisfied.

"And the moon charm, warlock!" he demanded. Todman smiled, thinly. He lifted the leather thong and its pendant bone and silver charm from around his neck, and threw it down at Wayland's feet contemptuously.

"Now we are equal," he sneered. The Green King flung back his cloak and took a stride forward.

"Let the combat begin!"

The warlock gave a great laugh as he leapt down from the stallion's back, confronting the Green King in the space between the unmoving Death Horse and the entrance to the tomb. For a moment, each man was perfectly still, poised and alert, in the manner of the temple wrestlers of ancient Greece. Then, with a joint grunt of mighty effort, they moved and met head-on; fingers locked, hand to hand, their thighs and sinews strained in desperate thrust, their necks bulged with the effort to overbalance the opponent and gain a swift advantage.

But this deadly match would not be easily won. Aged though Wayland was, his massive frame had the strength of seasoned oak; for all Todman's whipcord skill, the older man could not be turned or thrown. Even without the magic powers of his guardianship, he was an adversary to be feared; and as he wrenched his arm free of Todman's grip, he gave the warlock a blow that sent him reeling. Todman recovered on the instant and sprang at the aged smith, and blow for blow they struck home, again and again. Shuddering beneath the impact of those gnarled and knotted fists, Todman felt a sudden surge of fear; he must snatch the victory quickly, or he would quickly be the victim. This was home ground to the Green King and the old man could draw new strength from the very trees if needs be; Todman knew that, as the intruder, he had only his secret words of power to rely on, besides his own rapidly weakening muscles. Even as his mind fumbled for a plan he found himself hurled to the ground yet again. Painfully, he pulled himself onto all fours, and struggled for his breath, head down, eyes half-blinded by the sweat dripping from his brow.

It was then that he saw the chance of his salvation. On the grass beneath him was Wayland's hammer. It took only one glance up at the grim, advancing figure of Wayland to decide. There would be no mercy asked or granted here; and, with his life at stake, Todman made the forbidden move. Seizing the deadly tool of power, Todman lurched to his feet and extended it in a fierce gesture of command towards Wayland, stopping him in his tracks.

"Wayland!" he howled with cruel triumph, "The hammer is mine! Your reign is at an end!"

The Green King stood as though held by a mighty, invisible hand. His limbs no longer obeyed him, and only the tension in his majestic face showed his anger and dismay at Todman's treachery.

"No magic!" he cried out, but Todman only laughed. "The ancient law forbids it!"

"He who holds the hammer makes the law!" the warlock shouted. "Make ready to die, Old One – a new king waits to take your place!" With a savage gesture he ordered the helpless guardian to his knees. "Kneel before Todman the warlock," he snarled, and swung the hammer high above his head as he strode forward to stand over his still defiant victim, "for I am the future king! Zabaoth!…"

His eyes blazed, and he loomed over the Green King, poised for the downward blow that spelt oblivion.

"Firiel!…"

So intent was he on screaming out those final words of power that he did not see the priest-king's gesture that brought the Moon Stallion rearing high above the warlock's back.

"Samantas!"

Only at the third word of power did he hear a terrifying neigh, his death-knell, as a silvered hoof delivered the living thunderbolt that was his end.

*

Sam's horse reared wildly, neighing with panic, and the speeding trap slewed across the rutted track to end up, one wheel shattered, in the nearest ditch. Thrown to the ground, Purwell lay stunned and breathless, wondering what had happened. They had just swung round onto the steep track that would take them up Woolstone Hill onto the Ridgeway, when disaster had struck.

"Did y'hear that clap of thunder!" Sam exclaimed. "No wonder the old girl spooked!"

He went to the horse to see what could be done to free her. Purwell dusted himself down and stared accusingly at the cloudless sky.

"No sign of a storm," he muttered furiously, then turned in dismay to see the shattered trap. Nearby, Sam soothed the horse, which seemed unharmed.

"There's still a mile to go!"

"It's Shanks's pony then, sir," commiserated Sam, unhelpfully. "Daisy's all right, mind."

Purwell looked at the horse and saw it was his only chance of getting to Diana. He had never ridden bareback in his life, but at least the horse was trained to harness and had bit and bridle for control.

"The horse!" he snapped at Sam, "Get it free!"

"What?" answered the stable-boy, dimly wondering what the professor was on about.

"Take it out of the shafts!" insisted Purwell, searching for the straps and buckles to be freed. "I can ride it, man, don't you see? It's our only chance!"

*

With Estelle leading the way, she and Paul wheeled their horses at full gallop onto the Ridgeway. Giving them their heads, the two raced at breakneck speed along the verges of the broad chalk track. The thunderclap had unsettled them, too, as they reached the crest of Odstone Hill, but without a trap to add to the confusion they had managed to control their skittish horses and press on. Paul glanced up at the summery sky and frowned; the first mutter of thunder had been nothing to the later thunderclap, and a freak storm was the last thing they needed on a chase like this. Almost before he had time to worry further, Estelle had reached the opening in the hedgerow that formed the entrance to Wayland's Smithy, and rode into it. Paul followed, and watched enviously as the slim girl pulled her mount to a halt and slid down from the saddle all in one fluid movement. By the time Paul had clambered down, more clumsily, he found Estelle rooted to the spot, wide-eyed and dismayed, pointing wordlessly ahead.

Face down before the shadowed entrance to the burial chamber, Todman's lifeless body lay sprawled in a pose of abject, broken submission, as if hurled there by a gigantic hand. Apart from the limply spread-eagled corpse, the clearing was deserted; not even the singing of a bird disturbed the solitude. Estelle shivered slightly, and Paul was about to tell her to stay back, when she read his thought and with a determined tilt to her chin opened the gate and stepped into the glade ahead of him. Even so, she stopped short of the horse-master's crumpled body, and stood back as Paul crouched to pick up the broken moon charm from where it lay, just beyond the reach of Todman's dead fingers. He showed it to her, and, like Paul, she frowned. The talisman was scorched and splintered as if by the heat of an intense, unearthly fire.

Now they turned to stare down at Todman and again the youngsters looked back at one another, mystified. In the centre of that lifeless back there was another scorch mark, no bigger than a fist, between the shoulder blades.

"A crescent moon," muttered Paul, tracing its down-ward-pointing shape with a tentative finger.

"Or a horse shoe," Estelle countered, remembering the superstition; its luck poured away if you hung a shoe upside-down. Paul had just the same thought as he straightened from crouching over Todman.

"It's a sign of bad luck, isn't it?" he said grimly, then suddenly came alert, remembering why they had come to this eerie place. "Diana!" he called anxiously.

The sound was quickly lost among the trees set all around the glade like sentinels. There was only one place here to hide a prisoner, he thought, and looked towards the dark opening of the tomb. Gesturing to Estelle to stay back, he scrambled into the tiny forecourt and went inside. This time she obeyed him, weak at the thought at what he might find, but a second later he reappeared, concerned and puzzled.

"There's no sign of her," he said.

Estelle looked quickly all around the glade and realised that something else was missing: her father's horse.

"Rollo's not here either!" she exclaimed. "Perhaps Diana has used him to escape!" They looked at each other and hope grew; it was Rollo that had brought the blind girl home when Mortenhurze had died. Before they could work out why they hadn't passed horse or rider on their way up to the Downs, a nervous whinny came from the horses tethered at the gate.

"It's them!" cried Estelle and ran to see, but Paul

reached the chalk road outside before her. Their faces fell in disappointment; there was no one to be seen. Then a flicker of movement drew their gaze along the Ridgeway to the east. They stood, breathless and amazed. Hovering there, like a ghost amongst the distant shadows, was the Moon Stallion.

Chapter Sixteen

WHAT HAD PROMISED TO BE a straightforward task of releasing Daisy from the shafts of the broken trap was proving to be almost impossible. The harness on the shaft open to the lane was easy enough to get at, but the twisted fall had jammed the body of the trap firmly into the ditch and pulled the patiently waiting horse tight against the tangled hedge. The straps and buckles out of reach meant there was only one course left open for Sam and the professor, and it was Purwell who made the decision, ruthlessly.

"Cut the horse free, boy!" he ordered, and stepped back to watch as Sam reluctantly took out his clasp knife and opened the blade. The stable lad had barely put his hand on the first leather to be cut when Purwell's urgent call checked his movement. In the midst of mopping his perspiring forehead, the professor had found himself looking into the field beyond the lane, and what he saw there brought a muttered exclamation of amazement to his lips: a fine chestnut stallion, saddled but riderless, was grazing quietly not ten yards distant.

"Sam!" Purwell whispered sharply. "Is it Rollo?"

"It is, sir," came Sam's wondering reply, and he scratched his head in puzzlement. "The master's horse, God rest his soul." He turned to the professor at his side. "But what's he doing here?"

Purwell wasn't going to waste time answering questions; the opportunity seemed heaven-sent and he took it gladly.

"Will he come to you, Sam?" he demanded quietly.

"Aye, sir, he knows me well enough."

"Then get me on his back – and quickly!"

Sam took the horse cautiously, though he came quietly enough in the end. He was watched all the while by Purwell, who was nervously preparing himself for the ordeal of riding a mettlesome thoroughbred used only to the hand of an expert. Despite his attempts to dismiss Sam's question from his mind, it wouldn't leave him. A glance beyond the horse, as Sam brought it finally into the lane, revealed the sunlit west flank of White Horse Hill, hazy in the near distance. Had it been Todman's destination after all? Was he there now, with Diana as his prisoner?

"He's ready for you, sir!" called Sam, and Purwell went up to him. A clumsy scramble of arms and legs and he was on Rollo's back, fumbling for the stirrups, but the horse was already moving up the hill to where the rising lane met and crossed the Ridgeway.

"Hold him, sir!" Sam shouted. "Don't let him have his head!" The warning was of little use; the professor was already out of earshot and moving faster with every stride, though – as Sam noted with relief – his feet had found their grip at last. If he could only stay in the saddle long enough, he'd soon be at the crest of White Horse Hill; the mystery of it, to Sam's slow mind, was what Todman or the girl or anyone should hope to find atop that lonely, barren place…

*

Inside her head Diana sensed the awesome whisper that heralded the Wild Hunt and knew that Todman was destroyed. She stood to meet it, her feet uncertain on the grassy slope, her blind eyes facing out over the beaked head of the great chalk horse below her. As the sound and fury of the raging wind grew all around her, she understood its meaning; the spirit of the place sought only to protect itself, she must accept that. As though acknowledging the future mystery of the ancient hill, images welled up from her deepest mind, dark fragments of the vision shown to her by the priest-magician of the sacred grove: a blinding ball of fire that scorched all the living world around it to ashes… the desolation of a once-great, ruined city… a rusted car slewed and shattered on an empty highway… a winding stream of refugees, pausing to gaze upward at the sign of the chalk horse – and on the ridge above it, standing there as the blind girl stood there now, the Dark Rider. As before, he turned his head towards her as he sat in majesty upon the gleaming, moon-silvered stallion. Raising his mighty hand to the windy sky, the Dark Rider gave his final gesture of greeting.

Grim though he was, that sign meant hope; but now the wind rose to a terrifying chorus, as its invisible hooves raced from the sky across the naked hillside. Unseen hands plucked the cloak easily from Diana's helpless fingers, wordless voices screamed menace in her ears, a whirlwind of power pulled and dragged at her fail body and forced it back and back. She turned to seek some refuge from the lashing of that searing wind, but there was none; her stumbling feet caught on a tangling claw of grass and she fell to her knees. Even here the wind's anger forced her onwards, away from the safety of the grassy band and towards the narrow path that could lead only to destruction and the barren chalk far below. Kneeling, she cried out aloud into the screaming wind, a single desperate plea.

"Moon Stallion... help me!"

In that same moment, it was there, its sleek head nuzzling her shoulder. With a sob of relief, the blind girl stood, huddling tight and lacing her fingers into the richness of its windswept mane. But the pursuit wasn't over; still the storm-wind howled and shrieked at her, stunning her senses with its fury, snatching the breath from her parted lips, whipping her tangled hair across her desperate face. Suddenly she felt the stallion make its move; and, holding fast, Diana was forced to move with it... and she was afraid. Instead of leading her to safer, higher ground, the stallion was taking her *down* the slope, into danger, as if obeying the command of its avenging brotherhood, the Wild Hunt…

*

Only minutes before, after the first moment of astonishment, Estelle had felt a sullen rage that was almost revulsion; this was the wild white horse that her father had hunted for so long and which had in the end destroyed him. Her pretty face had hardened into anger as, facing Paul, she had rejected the promise always offered by the Moon Stallion but never granted.

"I don't care about it any more," she had told him, pleading with her eyes. "Don't let's chase it, Paul."

Paul understood her reasons and nodded in agreement; the stallion had caused more than enough trouble and heartache already. But then, just as he was about to turn away, he was forced to look again. The stallion walked towards them, then paused, waiting, as if for their response. Estelle saw it too, and wondered; but her memories were too bitter for her wonderment to last.

"What's it doing?" Paul asked her.

"It's taunting us," she answered, but found herself watching it, just the same. Again it trotted towards them, turned, and stood waiting. At last, Paul understood.

"Estelle, it wants us to follow!"

Dipping its head in silent acknowledgement, the stallion cantered away before pausing again, and now even Estelle was convinced. Eagerly she moved to her horse and mounted quickly.

"Hurry up, Paul!" she shouted as she urged Rex out onto the chalk avenue of the Ridgeway. "It's going to lead us to Diana!"

Within seconds the chase was on, heading furiously towards the grassy folds of Uffington Down and the earthen ramparts of its castle – only to be broken off in confusion as, coming out of the gap that crossed the slope of Woolstone Hill, Estelle almost collided with Rollo, carrying the professor headlong from the lane below. Barely managing to avoid the plunging tangle of bewildered horses, Paul recognised his father and called to him to ride on with them, but it needed Estelle's hand on Rollo's bridle before the chestnut stallion was calm again, and by then their guide had gone.

"Come on, Father – we're following the Moon Stallion!" shouted Paul, but almost immediately Estelle cried out in dismay.

"We've lost it!"

Paul was more confident and urged the others on, leaving any explanations for the gallop ahead. "Don't worry – we know where he was leading us!" he called back to the others, as they struggled to catch up with him. "To the White Horse!"

Unpractised rider though Purwell was, Rollo was soon matching Paul's horse stride for stride. The professor shouted across, his face serious and questioning.

"You found nothing, then?"

"Todman – dead." responded his son, bluntly. "No sign of Diana, though…"

Estelle urged Rex up to Rollo's shoulder, and called to Purwell, "Where was Rollo?"

"In a field – back there," explained the professor,

breathlessly. "He had no rider!"

"Diana *must* be up there!" The others followed Paul's stare ahead and rode on silently now, desperate to know the truth. The horses took the moat and grassy ramparts of the earthen fort of the great enclosure to the slope beyond that overlooked the great chalk image. Panting for breath, they reined in, looking urgently all about them. The hillside was utterly deserted; a whisper of wind swayed the taller stems of grass, but the rest was silence.

Suddenly Paul gave a muttered exclamation and clambered down from his horse. Running across the grass to a small dip in the bank, he snatched up Diana's cloak and held it for the others to see. None of them spoke; a dreadful apprehension gripped them all as they moved forward, grim-faced, to the edge of the slope that looked down on the altar that was Dragon Hill.

Where the body of Mortenhurze once sprawled there was only bare chalk. Purwell threw a quick glance at his son, his face tight with relief, and Paul answered with an anxious smile. Then suddenly Estelle was pulling at his arm and pointing, too choked to speak, at the barely visible beaked head of the chalk horse and its round white eye. Kneeling there, erect and calm, was Diana, her blind face turned towards them, filled with hope. With a whoop of joy, Purwell and his son ran down the slope, with Estelle directly at their heels, waving like exultant schoolchildren.

"Diana!" Purwell shouted, and she stood, a slow, serene smile making her face radiant as she answered him.

"Father?"

A moment later she was at the centre of a tangled, loving group, hugging and comforting each other in sheer delight, their shouts and greetings incoherent with relief and laughter.

"Thank God you're safe, child!" whispered Purwell into his daughter's hair, as he hugged her to him, not ashamed to cry as her gentle fingertips caressed his face. Paul bubbled over with excited laughter and cheerfully pulled Estelle into the heart of the family confusion.

"We've found you!" he yelled happily into his sister's loving face.

"Dear Diana," murmured Estelle, hugging the blind girl cheek to cheek, "we were so afraid for you."

"You'd no need to be." Diana pulled one arm free and pointed blindly to the hillside above them, her voice aglow with soft excitement. "Can't you see...?"

At the skyline was the wild white horse, touched with a sheen of pale May sunlight, motionless as the great chalk image that was guardian of so many secrets: the mysteries of the past, of the future, of the goddess whom they both served. A dip of its head in proud salute, and it turned away, as though in answer to Diana's blind gesture of farewell.

"Go safely, Moon Stallion," she whispered, and in that same instant it was lost to view, part of the wind that keened along the Ridgeway, subdued now, omniscient and ageless...